What More

Could You

Wish For

⤙ ❦ ⤚

What More Could You Wish For

Samantha Hoffman

St. Martin's Griffin
New York

This is a work of fiction. All of the characters, organizations, and events portrayed in this novel are either products of the author's imagination or are used fictitiously.

WHAT MORE COULD YOU WISH FOR. Copyright © 2012 by Samantha Hoffman. All rights reserved. Printed in the United States of America. For information, address St. Martin's Press, 175 Fifth Avenue, New York, N.Y. 10010.

www.stmartins.com

LIBRARY OF CONGRESS CATALOGING-IN-PUBLICATION DATA

Hoffman, Samantha.
    What more could you wish for / Samantha Hoffman.
— 1st ed.
        p. cm.
    ISBN 978-1-250-00303-4 (trade pbk.)
    ISBN 978-1-250-01581-5 (e-book)
  1. Self-realization in women—Fiction.   2. Marriage proposals—Fiction.   I. Title.
    PS3608.O4786W47 2012
    813'.6—dc23

                            2012004634

        First Edition: August 2012

        10 9 8 7 6 5 4 3 2 1

To my dad—my hero—who taught me to finish what I started and told me I could do anything I set my mind to. He would have been hugely proud to hold this book in his hands. He would have said to whoever was near: "My daughter wrote this."

But first he would have said to me, "Did you have to use all those swear words?"

What More Could You Wish For

One

Have you ever been at a party where the host comes up with some cutesy questions to kick things off? You know, like, *Who would you choose to be shipwrecked on a desert island with?* or *If you were a dog, what breed would you be?* or my personal favorite, *If you could turn back the clock, what age would you go back to?* I never even had to think about that one. I always said, "I wouldn't . . . I love the age I am."

Well, fuck that. Ask me now.

When you're twenty or thirty or even forty you can't imagine being fifty. But all of a sudden there it is, smacking you in the face, and all you can think is, How the hell did that happen? It's better, as they say, than the alternative. But really . . .

I thought if I ignored my fiftieth birthday it would go away, but Michael, my significant other, called on his way home from work, bursting my balloon of denial.

"Happy birthday, babe," he said. "So how does it feel to be fifty?"

"Well, you ought to know," I said.

"I ought to but it's too damn long ago. From where I'm

sitting, fifty looks like high school." One of the good things about being with someone older.

"It hardly feels like high school from where I'm sitting," I said. "Well, actually it doesn't feel that different, but then I go and do something stupid like look in the mirror."

"Oh, Libby, you look fine," Michael said.

"See?" I said. "That's what I mean. You used to think I looked hot. Now you think I look *fine*."

"Bad choice of word," Michael said. "I still think you're hot, you know that." Yeah, yeah, yeah, I thought. "Hey," he said, "why don't we go to that new sushi restaurant for dinner tonight?"

"We don't have to go out tonight," I said, thinking that crawling into bed and pulling the covers over my head would be the preferred alternative. "We're celebrating at my folks' tomorrow."

"I know, but it's not every day you turn fifty."

"Thank god," I said, examining myself in the mirror, face-lifting sagging skin with my free hand.

Michael and I had been together nearly two years. We weren't married; we didn't even live together. Some people thought it was an odd arrangement—that if we'd been together for that long we should just get married. But our deal—staying at each other's houses several times a week—worked for us. It wasn't just a toothbrush-in-the-bathroom trade-off. We had keys to each other's houses and clothes in each other's closets. I had makeup and hair products at his house; he had deodorant and nose-hair trimmers at mine. (You have to love a well-groomed man.) It was perfect for us, and many of my married friends sighed wistfully—actually sighed—when I talked about it. Anyway, Michael and I had a sweet, comfortable relationship, far more peaceful than any I'd been in before, including my two marriages.

I thought we'd spend the evening quietly at home with a nice bottle of Pinot Noir and my favorite Szechuan takeout, but Michael sounded so pleased with his sushi idea that I agreed. It was just dinner out, after all, not a party with big signs reading FIFTY IS THE NEW THIRTY. Because that's bullshit. It definitely is not.

I finished hemming one of the bridesmaid dresses I was working on for my best friend Sophie's daughter's wedding. Four duplicates hung on a rack like a chorus line at the Grand Ole Opry. I was eager to finish and get the purple extravaganzas out of sight. They clashed with the more subdued décor of the workroom, which was bright and crisp, but cozy and snug with soft pale yellow walls and nubby navy blue carpet. A large padded table filled the center space with my sewing machine at the end. One corner of the room was filled with a comfy two-person chair and ottoman and next to them were my desk, computer and some bookshelves. I loved the look of it, but I especially loved what it represented: my independence from the corporate world.

Now, while I waited for Michael to return phone calls and take a shower, I turned on my computer and double-clicked the AOL icon: "Welcome!" it said. "You've got mail!" I loved that. It was like winning a little prize, even if the prize was an e-mail from my mother.

Happy birthday, Libby. I can't believe you're 50! It makes me feel so old.

Tell me about it, I thought.

I'm making some of your favorite things for dinner tomorrow. Come over about 6.

> **By the way, I saw this article and thought you might be interested.**

She'd attached a link: *Retirement Planning for the Single Woman.* Jeez, AARP was already sending their damn magazine, wasn't that enough? Did I need this from my mother, too?

My mother couldn't grasp why I'd quit my job as a graphic designer and gone into business for myself. She never appreciated what I had done, how hard I'd worked at getting the word out: going to networking events, sending mailings to large apartment buildings in high-end neighborhoods, creating eBlasts. I suppose she worried my clients would dry up and I'd end up living in a cardboard box under an expressway. Or worse, at their house. But here I was, six years later, and business was thriving. I had a nice client list that helped me keep my hairstylist in business, stocked my cupboards with smoked oysters and good wine, and paid for vacations where I could drink foamy concoctions with tiny parasols and bendy straws. I was even putting money into a retirement fund, which I guess I needed to tell her.

I answered e-mails, checked an eBay auction, looked at some fashion sites and then just browsed, checking out the AOL welcome box with news briefs and weather forecasts and "Best Cities to Retire In." God, retirement was everywhere.

At the top of the page was a hyperlink for a website called SearchForSchoolmates.com and a picture of a girl who could have graduated in my high school class. She wore a dark turtleneck sweater with a locket on a small gold chain, and her long straight hair was parted down the middle. It was vintage seventies, exactly like my own senior picture. I smiled, thinking of my high school days of crowded halls, slamming lockers, the green shorts and white shirts we had to wear for gym class, and Mr. Pendergast, my French teacher, who I was sure would propose as soon as I had that diploma in hand. Me and every other girl in the class.

Of course I had to check out the website.

First I selected my state, then city, then high school and the year I graduated, and finally I entered my name, Elizabeth Carson. And voilà! Up came a list of 104 alumni from my graduating class. I laughed, looking at the familiar names: Mary Blevins, Susan Caldwell, Danny Schultz. I could picture Danny's blond hair and dazzling smile. Was he still cute, I wondered, or was he sporting a comb-over and forty extra pounds?

Page two was more of the same. Vague memories swam through my brain, of walking the locker-lined halls and sitting in classes passing notes to my friends. And homecoming and prom and the gymnastics competition. It had been thirty-two years since I'd seen any of these kids. The thought that these *kids* were fifty now was unimaginable.

I was on page three when it hit me. A name that made me sit back in my chair. *Patrick Harrison.*

Wow.

Patrick had been my first love. He was the bad boy with leather and long hair—the one my parents didn't like, the one I thought I couldn't live without. I could see us walking the tiled halls hand in hand, him dropping me at my classroom and kissing my eager lips before walking off to his own class. My heart would just about beat out of my chest. I thought I'd never survive until the hour passed and I could see him again. I clearly recalled that sweet terror, the heart palpitations, the blush that started at my chest and infused my whole body when I saw him walking toward me.

"Libby," Michael called now, "you about ready?"

"Be right there," I said and saved the SearchForSchool-mates.com website to my Favorite Places.

∾

Michael seized a piece of sushi with chopsticks and popped it into his mouth.

"Raw fish good," he said in his best caveman voice.

While we waited for our dessert, Michael told me about his new listings and a high-maintenance client he'd just started working with.

"Honestly, Lib, this guy would ask me to tie his shoelaces if he didn't wear loafers." Michael was one of the top real estate agents in the city. "So I show him three places; one's a short sale, one's a total gut-job and one's a straight foreclosure. . . ."

I admired his dedication, I really did, but he always gave me more details than my attention span had room for. So now I nodded and smiled and thought about Patrick Harrison, wondering what he was doing now. I couldn't imagine him as an attorney or an accountant. Definitely not a real-estate agent. I could see him as a forest ranger or maybe something in the nonprofit sector. Or maybe he was a fifty-year-old bike messenger pouring himself into spandex and still wearing a ponytail.

I knew I was going to send him an e-mail. But what would I say? *Hi, remember me? Remember when we slept together on New Year's Eve when we were seventeen?*

I was in the middle of doing the depressing math on that one when the waitress brought two tulip-shaped glass dishes, each containing a perfect scoop of green-tea ice cream. Mine had a sparkler twinkling in the middle.

"Happy birthday," she and Michael said in unison. I braced

myself for them to break into an off-key rendition of the song and let out a relieved breath when they didn't. I pulled out the sparkler and we both dug in, remarking how yummy it was—how cold and creamy. Then Michael put down his spoon, reached into his pocket and placed a small velvet box in front of me. I blinked.

"Open it," he said, pushing it closer.

I stared. I had a bad feeling. It was surely a ring but hopefully it was a cocktail ring or even a mood ring. Trepidation swirled around my throat.

The waitress and two busboys stood watching from a respectful distance, grinning like kids with a new Game Boy. "Go on," Michael said.

What could I do? Refuse? So while everyone watched I gingerly lifted the little lid. There, like a searchlight, sat an enormous diamond ring. My mouth fell open. The waitress clapped her hands together.

"Will you marry me, Libby?"

Marry him? Really? I studied his face hoping he was kidding, but he watched me eagerly.

What was he thinking? Fifty percent of all marriages fail. Not to mention one hundred percent of mine. "My god, Michael, it's huge," I said. What I wanted to say was, *What the fuck, Michael? If you wanted to get married, couldn't we have talked about it privately instead of turning it into a spectacle?* "How could I wear this? It's bigger than my fist," I said. He laughed. "You shouldn't have bought this. I'm too old for an engagement ring."

And I don't want to marry you.

"You're never too old for diamonds," he said.

Well, of course I knew that, but still. . . .

I noticed then that the only sound in the restaurant was the faint clanking of dishes from the kitchen; I looked around to find five or six tables of patrons watching me. A plump, gray-haired woman in a flower-print blouse smiled encouragingly. A small blond girl with a pink feather in her hair sat on her knees, arms crossed on the back of the chair. It was like a stage play, and Michael was enjoying his role as the romantic male lead. What was I supposed to do now? How could I say anything other than yes with all these people watching?

"Put it on," he said. I hesitated. "Go ahead." I took it out of the box. I made a show of it being too heavy to lift and Michael and our little audience laughed. When I slid it on my finger his eyes sparkled and he leaned forward.

"Well?" he said. "Will you?"

I held up my hand and made another show of being blinded by the glitter. When in doubt, play to the crowd. I was just stalling, of course, trying to think what to do. Trying to think of how to kill Michael in front of all these witnesses. I had a quick vision of taking off the ring, putting it safely in Michael's hand, then running like hell out of the restaurant and maybe going into witness protection. But I took the coward's way out.

"How could I not want to marry a man who would buy a ring like this?" I said. Not a yes, I reasoned. An answer I could explain away later when I told him what I really meant was *no*.

The waitress let out a little squeak and there was a smattering of applause.

"Did you pay these people?" I asked.

Michael's smile illuminated his face like a sunrise. He came around to my side of the table and put his arms around me, pulled me close. "I love you, Libby," he said and kissed me.

I kissed him back and waited for the tingle—the blush, the thrill I'd felt with Patrick Harrison so many years ago. It didn't come. What I felt instead was like a solid mass of cement sitting on my chest.

Shit.

"You've made me a very happy man," Michael said, his eyes crinkling with pleasure. "We'll have a great life together." He laughed. "Well, we already do, but somehow it feels different now. Don't you think?"

"Yes," I said. "It definitely feels different."

Two

---❧ ❦ ❧---

I'd never seen Michael as animated as he was on the short ride home. It was a little unnerving. Typically he was a relaxed and steady guy, not emotional or showy but calm, quietly intelligent and reliable. But I could only describe what he was doing now as chattering like a kid instead of a fifty-nine-year-old man. Had his sushi been laced with magic mushrooms?

"So I Googled 'best jewelers Chicago' and picked five or six and then I read all the reviews and then I Googled 'diamonds' and found out about the four Cs of diamond buying"—he looked over at me—"cut, clarity, color, carat," he finished proudly.

I didn't want to encourage him, but I couldn't resist. "So how many carats?"

"Three." He smiled. "I would have gone bigger," he said, "but the jeweler convinced me that since your hands are small, a larger diamond would overwhelm them."

Maybe my hands weren't overwhelmed but the rest of me sure was.

He continued the chatter. I would have been amused if I

didn't hate the whole situation so much. I sat silent, cowed by his enthusiasm, feeling backed into a corner. How could I tell him I didn't want to marry him, that I didn't want to get married at all? I'd already been married, twice, and it hadn't worked for me. Michael had always said he understood, that he was fine with it. What the hell had happened here? Now, amazingly, he was under the impression I'd said I would marry him and he was excited, as excited as I'd ever seen him. How could I break it to him? It felt cruel to throw cold water on such unbridled enthusiasm.

At my house he pulled me into his arms and told me again how happy I'd made him.

"Michael . . ." I began, feeling the walls closing in.

"I know, I know," he said, laughing. "I'm acting like a schoolboy, aren't I? But I can't help myself, Lib, I'm so happy."

Oh god. I couldn't do it. I couldn't bring myself to be the dasher of his dreams. I couldn't bear the thought of his disappointment. I'll tell him tomorrow, I thought, in the light of a new day, when he's back to his normal, rational, sensible self.

ᴡ

Once I woke from a dream in complete and utter panic. Holy shit, I had thought, and grabbed my head because I'd dreamed that someone shaved me bald. Well, that's how I felt when I woke the next morning, like I'd had a bad dream. I was ready to evacuate the whole thing from my mind but then I rolled over and there was that small velvet box, like a cockroach on my nightstand. *Crap.*

So I waited, whether for a feeling of euphoria or a modicum of enthusiasm I didn't know. But neither came. What did come was dismay. I didn't want to turn over for fear I would see Michael's face, all eager and elated, wanting to talk about a wedding: who we'd invite, what we'd serve, how much an open bar would cost. I didn't want to discuss any of that. In my mind I could see a room full of smiling friends and relatives, and then I saw my middle-aged self in a tea-length dress trying to remember to keep my stomach sucked in as I picked up reading glasses from a chain around my neck to read my vows.

When I finally worked up the courage to look, I was relieved to find the bed empty except for Rufus, my cat, who ambled over and plopped his considerable mass next to me for his morning scratch. I lay for a moment lavishing attention on Rufus before getting out of bed to see what Michael was up to. But he wasn't there. He'd left a note on the kitchen counter.

To my fiancée,

He'd drawn a smiley face here. A *smiley face.*

I went to play racquetball, then I have a couple of showings, then a meeting this afternoon at the office. I might be a little late—might have to meet you at your parents' house as close to six as I can. I'll call you later.
   I love you.

I did what I always do in times of crisis: called Sophie, who'd been my best friend since we were fourteen.

"I was just going to call you," she said. "Happy birthday. I'm so glad you're older than me. So how does it feel to be fifty?"

"You'll find out for yourself in three months, and you're not going to like it."

"Three *long* months," she said. "And I'm going to lord that over you every second."

"I know you will. You live for those pitiful months," I

said. "Hey, you know how Michael and I always say how much we like our arrangement; having our own places but spending half the week together, being committed but happily unmarried?"

"Okay, are you trying to make me jealous just because I'm younger than you?"

I laughed. "Well, get this: Michael proposed last night and gave me a three-carat diamond."

Silence. "Soph?" I said.

"Holy shit," she said. "Well, that's great. I'm excited. Just don't make me wear a pink dress with puffy sleeves again."

She'd been my maid of honor twice, but only once in pink. Both times in puffy sleeves, though.

"I don't think I want to get married."

"You said no to *three carats*?"

"Not exactly." I told her about the evening, how I'd felt railroaded into saying yes.

"Well, give it some more thought before you do anything. Don't get hung up on the way he did it. He was just being romantic."

"Michael's not exactly a romantic guy."

"I always thought he had it in him. Think about it a little, Lib. Maybe third time's the charm."

"Or not. Maybe three strikes and you're out."

"You can't count the first two," she said. "You married Jeremy when you were twenty, too young to know what you were doing."

"You were twenty-one when you married Pete and you're still married," I pointed out.

"I was always more mature," she said. "Besides, we're not talking about me. So, scratch Jeremy. Then you married Wally on the rebound, so he doesn't count either. Michael counts. He's not like either of them. He'll be a great husband."

"How so?"

"He's solid, responsible, nice looking, kind. Should I go on?" She didn't wait for my reply. "Generous, sweet, smart, everyone loves him . . ."

"Okay, so I'll manage his political campaign."

"He's a good guy and he'd do anything for you and you get along great. What more could you wish for?"

"Shining armor? A white horse?"

"Oh, hon, that's for kids. And that stuff doesn't last anyway."

"So now I don't get passion, I get peace instead, is that the idea? Security instead of excitement? Comfort instead of romance?"

"Something like that."

"Is that what happens when you're fifty?"

"It's what happens, period. It's what you end up with anyway, if you're lucky. It's nice, Lib."

"Nice? Seems pretty boring to me."

"This doesn't sound like you. What's this all about? You're crazy about Michael."

"I am," I said. "Michael's great. We have a nice relationship and it's nice the way it is. But marriage? I don't know. I don't exactly have that can't-live-without-him kind of feeling."

I'd never had that with Michael, not even when we first met. It wasn't that I didn't like being with him or didn't look forward to seeing him. I did, of course, but I never had that frantic will-he-call-me-does-he-like-me kind of craziness. And I liked that. It made things so much simpler.

❦

I met Michael at a 5K race. The weather had been warm that day, but a soft drizzle was coming down and the skies looked like they might open up any minute. Since the race was only three miles, the runners seemed pretty motivated to clock a fast time before the downpour. The gun went off and we started the scenic course through the park and around the lake. I went out too fast as I usually do when I race, getting caught up in the excitement and competition. My legs and lungs were feeling the stress of my effort by the second mile and I slowed a bit to take in more air. A few people passed me, which always annoyed me, especially toward the end of a race, but I didn't have it in me to kick it up. Then two women passed, one much younger than I but the other a woman in my age group, someone I often saw at various races and who always finished ahead of me. She wore a red baseball cap and her ponytail waved like a hand through the vent in the back. If I increase my pace just a little, I thought, I can beat this woman for once, place in my age group and win a medal. The last half mile was a straightaway and when I saw the banner across the finish line far in front of me I knew I could do it, so I set my sights on that banner and kicked into gear.

There was one last water stop on my right, a long table with volunteers wearing blue Windbreakers handing out plastic cups of water. Discarded cups littered the ground. I did a little dance step to avoid a bouquet of them in front of me and landed wrong, twisting my ankle as I went down.

I crumpled to my knees in pain, people running past me, a blur of colorful racing clothes and bib numbers. Red Cap's ponytail waved goodbye as she moved confidently toward the finish line.

"Shit."

Several people from the water stop ran over to help, one a wiry guy with thin, gray hair and a mustache, a take-charge kind of guy, older than the others. "I've got it covered," he told them and sent everyone back to man the table. He checked my ankle expertly, his manner no-nonsense and professional.

"It doesn't feel like you broke anything," he said. "Probably just a sprain. But you might want to have it X-rayed in any case."

"I'm fine," I said brusquely, then nearly collapsed again as I put weight on the foot. That's when the skies opened up. Big time. Like someone had turned on a spigot. Within seconds we were drenched.

"Let me help you," he said, and supported me as I hobbled to the finish line, where a tent was set up with Gatorade and bagels. Once we were under cover, he deposited me in a corner away from the stomping feet of the finishers and went to get some dry towels and an ACE bandage. Nice-looking man, I thought, as I watched him rummage efficiently through the boxes. I liked his competence.

"Here," he said, handing me a plastic bag filled with ice. "You need to keep that on your ankle for about half an hour and then we'll wrap it in the ACE bandage. You should elevate it, too, if we can find something to prop your leg on." He looked around the tent, grabbed a plastic milk crate and positioned it under my leg with the ice pack.

"Are you a doctor?" I asked.

"No, no. But I've sprained my share of ankles." He smiled and put out his hand. "Michael Dean," he said.

"Elizabeth Carson." I shook his hand.

"If it hurts a lot or the swelling gets intense, it could be a fracture."

"I'm sure it'll be fine. I appreciate your help. Glad you were there."

"Well, I'm glad *you* were there. Not glad you sprained your ankle, but you did save me from standing out in that downpour."

I laughed, conscious now of how I looked with my dripping hair plastered to my head like seaweed. "Well, glad to be of assistance." I was starting to come down from my frustration and disappointment. It was only a race after all, and there were races every weekend. "You look like a runner," I said. "How come you're not running in this?"

"My running days are behind me. Bad knees. Now I just volunteer. Trying to get a contact runner's high, I guess."

He was gentle as he wrapped my ankle, winding the bandage tightly and fastening it with that little silver gizmo. Then he helped me to my feet.

"How does it feel?" he asked as I put a little weight on it.

"Not too bad." I looked up at him. "Thanks again for your help."

"Do you need a lift home?"

"No. I appreciate it but I've got my car here."

"Okay," he said. "I guess since it's your left ankle I have to let you drive."

"Well, thanks for your help, Doc," I said.

He laughed and put out his hand. "It was nice meeting you, Elizabeth."

"Libby," I said. His grasp was firm but gentle, his hand warm. "It was nice meeting you, too." I started to go but he held on to my hand, and I turned to look at him questioningly, at his friendly eyes and warm, kind smile.

He hesitated, just the briefest moment, and then asked, "Would you like to have dinner sometime, Libby? Or are you married?"

"Not married," I said, and happiness floated over his expression. "I'd love to have dinner sometime."

So we did—sushi, it turned out—and Michael was charming. He was great company; easy to talk to and attentive, with lovely manners and a quick laugh. My heart didn't palpitate when I looked into his brown eyes, but I felt safe and relaxed with him. I was enormously attracted by his affability and thoughtfulness, and our life together ever since had had a comforting orderliness to it.

My friends and family loved Michael and thought he was the perfect guy for me, which normally would have sent me running in the other direction, but this time I thought perhaps they were right. Our relationship seemed *adult* to me. I guess I thought that was what happened when you were older, and I liked it.

Then.

"Well, think about it," Sophie said now. "Is there anything you can't live without at this stage in your life? Or any*one*? We're not kids anymore. Think about your future. Think about what it would be like if you didn't have someone to share your life and grow old with."

"I do think about that." I pictured me and Rufus sitting in a rocking chair in a dim room that smelled of peppermint and cat food. "I haven't said no," I told her. "You're right, I do need to give it more thought. I will. Just don't tell anyone yet, okay? Not even Pete."

"I won't," she said.

Yeah, right.

Three

─୨ ᴪ ୧─

It was a beautiful morning. I laced up my running shoes and headed out through the neighborhood toward the forest preserve path. The sky was a clear pale blue with feathered clouds off in the distance. I pulled the freshness into my lungs and relished the peace. The air smelled pure, like pine and sunshine, and felt cool on my skin.

It was early and silent. Newspapers still lay rolled up on porches and stoops. One rested on top of a shrub. I loved my neighborhood with its mature trees and houses that weren't cookie cutter, unlike the new, treeless housing developments. Mostly the houses here were bungalows in varying styles— some Queen Anne, some Prairie, many with dormers and leaded glass. Every so often there was one in need of a little TLC, but generally they were well tended with tidy yards.

As I got closer to the forest preserve, the houses changed in style, becoming a bit larger, more elegant. On Cherry Street I ran past my favorite: a white, two-story colonial with a wraparound porch, a white picket fence, lace curtains, and window boxes that were filled with bright red geraniums in the summertime. It was right out of *Father Knows Best*. I'd never seen any signs of life, but imagined the woman of the house in a blue shirtwaist with an apron and pearls, serving piping-hot pancakes with big fat squares of melting butter to her smiling, fresh-faced family.

You couldn't help but be happy in a house like that. I'd always thought that if a For Sale sign went up I'd buy it and live happily ever after with the ready-made family who would move in with me. Now, at fifty, that fantasy needed readjustment.

The forest preserve path was peaceful when I reached it, with just a couple of other runners. Michael didn't like me to run this path. He thought it dangerous for a woman alone and said I should run on streets where there were people and cars. But it always felt safe to me, and tranquil, so I just didn't tell him that I did it.

I thought about what Sophie had said, that I needed to give Michael's proposal serious thought before making a decision. It *would* be nice to grow old with someone. I *did* want that. But for some reason it was hard to envision living with Michael, let alone being married to him, and what did that say about our relationship? In all the time we'd been together we'd only talked once or twice about getting married, and then just briefly.

The first time was after we'd been together a couple of months. We'd gone downtown for brunch at Luxbar and then taken a walk up North State Parkway, stopping in front of the yellow rowhouses just north of Division. They were gorgeous. Most of Michael's business was in the suburbs of Chicago, but occasionally he got a listing downtown. And he knew a lot about the buildings and the architecture.

"These row houses were built in 1875, Lib," he told me. "They're spectacular historic buildings and they've all been modernized. Really amazing. I saw one a couple years ago on a Realtor's tour. Incredible."

"You should buy one," I said. "What a great place to live."

"I think they're a bit over my budget." He'd looked at me. "But if you went in on it with me . . ."

I'd laughed. "I could maybe afford the first-floor bathroom."

He put his arm around me as we walked on, admiring the brownstones with their wrought-iron balconies and huge bay windows.

"Have you ever thought about living downtown?" Michael asked.

"I have, actually. I'd love to. Just not sure I could afford it. How about you?"

"Yeah, I think I would. I don't think I'd want to do it by myself, but it would be nice to start a new adventure with someone by my side." He looked at me and smiled, raising his eyebrows Groucho Marx style. "Ya know what I mean?"

I smiled. What *did* he mean? Was he thinking we should move in together? *Already?*

"Do you think you'd ever get married again?" he asked.

Holy crap.

I stopped and turned to face him, forcing his arm to slip off my shoulder. "Whoa, slow down," I'd said. "You're going to give me a heart attack here." I chuckled, but really, he was freaking me out.

He studied me, I suppose to see if I was kidding. "Relax," he said. "I'm not proposing. Honest. Just making conversation."

"Whew!" I said. "Let's save this conversation for another time, okay? Maybe when we know more about each other than our favorite restaurant and what kind of vodka we prefer."

"I feel like I *do* know you," he'd said. "It feels like I've known you for a long time." He squeezed my hand. "But don't worry, I'm not suggesting we elope or anything."

"Well thank god, because I have nothing to wear." We continued walking, sunlight peeking through the trees, wind chimes tinkling. It was a clear, crisp day.

"I have to warn you," I said. "I'm a bit cynical about marriage. Relationships in general, I suppose. I've been married twice already and they didn't take. I'm not chomping at the bit to give it another shot." It wasn't news to him that I was a two-time loser but I thought it bore repeating.

"That's cool," he'd said. "I hear you. And I don't want to scare you. It's not that marriage is a big deal to me, but I guess something long term is." He squeezed my hand. "And I'm not pushing that either. Time will tell, won't it?"

He didn't bring up marriage again for a long time, and when he did, the conversations were always casual, not marry-me-or-else kind of conversations. In the meantime we'd settled in and had a nice, effortless life together as well as our lives apart. It worked for us. It was good, and it took some anxiety out of the relationship that there was no pressure to change our status, that neither of us was worrying about what the other was thinking. And Michael had seemed content with the status quo.

Until yesterday.

Now my feet made a soft *thump, thump, thump*ing sound on the dirt path. Leaves swayed in the light breeze. I thought about how I'd felt with Patrick Harrison so many years ago. There's a huge difference between being seventeen years old and being fifty, I knew that. I was light-years beyond that kind of adolescent frenzy, but I really wished I felt some of the passion, had just a smidgeon of that out-of-control feeling I'd had back then.

In all the excitement I'd forgotten to tell Sophie about see-ing Patrick's name on SearchForSchoolmates.com. She'd get a kick out of it. His was one of those names we'd often bring up in our nostalgic "Remember the time . . ." conversations.

I thought about the first time I'd seen Patrick, at a Christ-mas party my senior year in high school. I'd been talking to Sophie and Pete, who was then her boyfriend, and I'd whis-pered, "Who's that?" when Patrick walked in. He wore black jeans and a black leather jacket with a silver chain hanging from his pocket. His hair was long, past his shoulders, much longer than the other guys wore it. Longer, even, than mine. He looked dangerous to me, and very sexy.

Pete had waved him over and I'd stared at Sophie. "You *know* him?" She'd smiled.

"Patrick, this is Libby," Pete had said. Patrick's eyes were soft and brown, and he looked at me in a way no boy ever had before, as if he recognized me from somewhere. It made me feel like I was the only girl in the room. I was appalled to feel myself blushing, but he smiled and took my hand, send-ing a tingle up my arm.

He said, "Is it corny to say that you are truly beautiful?"

"No!" Sophie said at the same time Pete said, "Yes," and we all laughed. The air around us shimmered as the music pounded. "Come on," Patrick said, "let's dance." He guided me into the middle of the crowd and we spent the rest of the evening together. Later, when I was in danger of missing my curfew, Patrick drove me home and I sat right up against him on the bench seat of his big black Ford.

Before I got out of the car he put his arm around me and kissed me softly. Then he looked directly into my eyes and said, "So . . . do you want to be my girlfriend?"

"I do," I said. And we both had laughed delightedly.

❦

When I got home from my run I went immediately to my computer, without even taking off my sweaty clothes. I pulled up SearchForSchoolmates.com and clicked on Patrick's name. In order to send an e-mail I had to sign up and pay fifty dollars. *Fifty bucks?* I hesitated for about two and a quarter seconds. Finally there was the e-mail window with Patrick's name in the To box and mine in the From.

Patrick, I began.

> **I have no idea what made me go to SearchForSchool-mates.com, but when I saw your name on the list it made me smile and I had to join just so I could e-mail you. So you owe me $50!**
>
> **How is it possible that it's been 32 years?**
>
> **I have so many fond memories of you. I remember your black leather jacket and your great smile. I remember dancing to Aerosmith and Badfinger. And I remember New Year's Eve at Jack Bradshaw's house when we were 17. Whenever anyone asks me about my most memorable New Year's Eve, that's the one I describe.**
>
> **What's happened in your life? Last I heard (20some years ago) you had moved to Florida. Are you still there?**
>
> **I hope you haven't forgotten me—I would be crushed.**
> **I hope you are well.**

I signed it, wrote *Your past comes back to haunt you* in the subject line and read it over again. Should I send it? If I did would I tell Michael? Somehow that didn't seem likely. But what the hell, I thought, and before I could change my mind, clicked Send.

I laughed at the nervousness I felt. What was that all about? Who cared? He was just a guy I'd known a lifetime ago. Big deal if I never heard from him.

But I hoped I would. I hoped he'd write back and say he thought about me every New Year's Eve at midnight. I hoped that night was indelibly etched in his brain as it was in mine. It was the night, after all, that I lost my virginity.

Four

—◦❦◦—

I'd been ecstatic when Patrick asked me out for New Year's
Eve. We'd only been dating a few weeks and it was such a
big-deal date night. We'd go to a house party, he said, and I
imagined us in a room full of other kids, dancing when midnight struck, his face close to mine, and then he would kiss
me. Would it be a slow, passionate kiss in front of all those
people, or just a peck? A sweet, lingering one, I hoped. One
that announced that I was his.

"It's at Jack Bradshaw's house," he told me. I'd known Jack
since third grade. Our fathers played softball together, our
mothers played bridge. Patrick told me Sophie and Pete would
be there but he didn't know who else. That didn't matter a
whit to me. All I cared about was being with Patrick.

Sophie and Pete were already at Jack's when we arrived
that night, and Jack's friend Frank, but no one else. Were
we early? A table was laden with chips, sour cream and onion dip, cocktail weenies wrapped in pastry, and Cheetos.
Lots of Cheetos. A cooler with beer and ice stood on the
floor in front of the table. It appeared that nothing had been
touched except for the two Pabst Blue Ribbons that Jack

and Frank held. The Doors blasted from the stereo with "Light My Fire."

"Where is everyone?" Patrick asked as he shook hands with Jack and Frank.

"We're it," Jack said over the music. "Everyone else had something else going on. Said maybe they'd stop by later." Clearly this was not his first beer. "Frank and I are going out. You guys are welcome to stay. No one's home, folks are out—won't be back till the wee hours of the morning. Eat, drink, be merry. We'll be back later." And then they were gone. The four of us burst out laughing.

So there we were, seventeen years old, alone in an empty house. Pete and Patrick each grabbed a frosty beer, clinked bottles, and took a long swallow. Then they got beers for me and Sophie.

"What the hell happened here?" Pete asked.

"How is it *everyone* had something else going on?" I asked. "When did he ask them? *This afternoon?*"

"Well, hey," Patrick said, "here we are in this big ol' house with food, beer, music and"—he looked at me—"each other. Can't get much better than that."

"I'll drink to that," Pete said, and we all clinked beer bottles.

There was a huge stack of LPs by the stereo and we looked through Jack's collection. He had all our favorites: Creedence Clearwater Revival, Bad Company, Steely Dan, the Moody Blues, Neil Young. We talked and laughed and listened to music. We danced to the rock stuff and a little later turned down the lights and put on some slow songs. It was cozy and warm in the basement rec room, and having Patrick's arms around me made it even warmer. He held me close and kissed the top of my head. I loved the feel of his body skimming mine and the way he ran his hands up and down my back. I wrapped my arms around him and closed my eyes. It was a perfect New Year's Eve.

Sophie and Pete made out as they danced and I couldn't help watching them over Patrick's shoulder. I envied how easy they were with each other. Before long they disappeared entirely. After a while Patrick looked around the room and said into my ear, "Hmmmm, looks like we're all alone."

I was thrilled. And scared. We sipped our beer and danced some more and then Patrick kissed me, baby kisses on my neck and forehead. Then he kissed my mouth. His lips were soft and his tongue was in my mouth and there was no one to watch us and the house was quiet except for Elton John on the stereo. The lights were low and we sat on the couch, sinking into the puffy cushions.

His kisses were silky and his hands roamed my back and shoulders and up into my hair, making me tingle. When his hand found my breast, a part of me no one had ever touched before, I couldn't concentrate on the kissing. But I didn't stop him. I liked it, even while a voice in my head told me I shouldn't let him do this, that it wasn't right, that we hadn't known each other long enough and he would think I was easy. Things were different then from how they are now; kids weren't so sophisticated, things didn't move so fast, relationships were more chaste, at least until you were an established couple. At least for good girls. I worried, but I'd had too much beer to worry for long.

Patrick moaned a little. Then he took my hand and said, "Come on," pulling me off the sofa and leading me upstairs, into one of the bedrooms.

"Should we be in here?" I asked, wanting to stall, wanting to run out the door and into the street and right home to the safety of my father's house.

"Sure. It's okay," he said. He locked the door and said, "All safe now. Is that better?" Not really, I thought, but I didn't want to be a prude.

Patrick pulled back the flowered bedspread and sat down while I stood, not knowing what to do or say. I felt conspicuous and awkward, and I thought I should get the hell out of there before I did something I'd regret. Actually, I was eyeing the door for a quick getaway when he patted the bed beside him and said, "Come here," so irresistibly that I went right over, as if magnetized, and sat beside him.

I stared at my hands. "I'm not sure we should do this," I said, thinking he would laugh at me.

"It's okay," he said. "We won't do anything you don't want to do."

He brushed my hair behind my ear and kissed it. His tongue darted inside and sent a thrill up my spine. Then he kissed my neck and buried his face in my hair.

"Smells nice," he murmured. I started to relax and soon his hand was on my breast again. I kissed him back, touching his chest and running my fingers through his soft, silky hair. His hand snaked up under my sweater and caressed my breasts over my bra, and then he pushed my bra aside and touched my nipples, sending electricity up my spine.

His breathing was faster now. So was mine.

As if I had done it countless times before, I sat up, feeling bold, pulled my sweater over my head and removed my bra with a quick, expert movement. Suddenly there I was, practically naked. Oh, Jesus. It was like I was possessed.

Patrick gazed at me—into my eyes, at my hair, my mouth, my breasts—and then he got up on his knees and took his shirt off, pushed me gently onto my back and lay down directly on top of me, his smooth, narrow chest connecting with mine, his skin cool. His back felt strong and muscled. I was breathless under him. But uncertain, afraid.

"Patrick . . ." I said.

He stopped, looked at me. "What, darlin'? You okay?" The warmth of his sincerity melted my hesitation like butter.

"I'm okay," I whispered, and he planted kisses all over my neck and shoulders and breasts.

There was an awkward moment as he started to pull off my bell-bottoms. I helped him by lifting my hips off the bed and I could feel my face color. He didn't seem to notice. He stood, leaving me exposed, alone and naked on the bed. He looked at me while he took off his jeans and Jockey shorts and I pretended I wasn't embarrassed, making an attempt to look sexy (whatever that was) and returning his stare, resisting the impulse to pull the bedspread over my nakedness. I could see peripherally that his penis was jutting straight out from his body, and it was so weird that I had to fight the urge to laugh. I desperately wanted to examine it but couldn't bring myself to look at it directly. Then I thought, How will that thing fit inside me?

He pulled something out of his jeans pocket and when the wrapper crinkled I knew it was a condom. Oh my god, I thought, I am really doing this. By then there was no part of me that didn't want to, but it felt surreal. Patrick returned to lie beside me and pulled me back into his arms. He was unhurried and careful, as if I were a baby bird, and when he entered me he was gentle and cautious. "Is this your first time?" he asked. I couldn't speak. I couldn't catch my breath. I nodded. "Are you okay?" he asked one more time, and I nodded again.

Don't ask me any more questions, I thought, just do it. And he did. And it hurt for a moment but then it didn't, and

I could feel him inside me, pulsing and warm and I thought, I have a penis inside me.

Bells didn't ring and fireworks didn't explode, but when Patrick looked at me with those penetrating, sparkly eyes, it made my heart smile.

Afterward, we lay side by side, my head in the crook of his shoulder. He stroked my arm as his breathing slowed, and then he turned over, his arm forming a tripod to hold his head as he looked at me and asked, "Was it good for you?"

"It was great," I said. And it was, but not for the reasons Patrick assumed. It was great because it made me feel special inside, and loved, and very grown-up.

"You're beautiful, Libby," Patrick said as he swept wisps of hair off my forehead. That was the part I liked best, more than the sex act itself—that attentiveness, those small but weighty gestures that made me feel valued. My heart wanted to lift right out of my body and float around the room. I wanted him to say it again. I wanted him to say he loved me.

Patrick got up out of bed, took my hand and pulled me up with him. When I stood he held my arm out to the side and his eyes traveled over every inch of my body. I didn't flinch as he admired me. "Beautiful," he said. "Perfect."

I blushed.

"Dance with me," he said, and took me in his arms. There was no music but my heart sang so loudly I thought that was what he must have heard.

I was in heaven. Pure heaven.

And then someone pounded on the door.

"Who's in there?" Jack Bradshaw shouted, his voice edged with panic. "Harrison, is that you?"

"Uh, yeah. Just a minute," Patrick called as we frantically grabbed our clothes off the floor, my heart pounding like a jackhammer.

"C'mon, man, get outta there. Now! My parents are pulling into the garage!"

Thinking back on this now made me chuckle, but there had been nothing funny back then. We'd both been horrified.

I was eating pancakes the next morning when Jack's mother called. My mom picked up the phone in the kitchen and my fork froze in midair when she said, "Margie, happy new year to you, too." *Jack Bradshaw's mom.*

I watched her face and saw the exact moment when Mrs. Bradshaw described what she had seen last night after Patrick and I threw on our clothes and sprinted out of the bedroom— buttoning, zipping, tucking in. Mrs. Bradshaw had smiled at first as we came rushing down the stairs, about to say, "Happy new year," until she took in the scene and our disarray, and her eyes went flat.

"Libby," she had said. "What's going on here?" Although it was clear as air.

My mother turned to me and stared as she listened, her eyes saturated with disappointment. "Don't move," she said when she hung up. And then she left the kitchen.

This must be what it feels like to go to the guillotine, I'd thought, cutting my pancakes into tiny pieces, pouring more syrup on top and mashing it all with my fork. By the time my parents came back and sat at the table, I was looking at a big gluey mass. My mother eyed the plate.

"Mrs. Bradshaw says you and Patrick used their bedroom last night and left it a shambles," she said.

"It wasn't a *shambles*," I said.

"So you *were* in their bedroom?" my father said. I couldn't bear the disapproval in his eyes. I picked up the fork and mashed some more.

"Libby, explain yourself."

How could I possibly do that?

"Oh, Libby," my mom said. "Tell me you were just making out."

Hearing the words "making out" coming from my mother's lips grossed me out.

Mash. Mash. Mash.

"For Christ's sake, is that the kind of girl you are?" my dad said. He sat down and shook his head. "I'm shocked, I really am."

"You *slept* with that boy," my mother said.

Mash. Mash. Mash.

"Sex is serious, Libby," she said. "Sex should be something special between two people who love each other and want to build a life together."

"Do you know what boys your age think about girls who have sex with them?" my father said, and I wanted to clap my hands over my ears and hum to drown out whatever words would follow.

"You're too young to have sex," my mother said. "You have no idea what you're doing, what that means."

"I do, too. I'm not an idiot, I'm *seventeen*," I said. "And I don't go around having sex with all the boys at school."

"Well, thank god for that," my mom said.

"And who is this boy? We don't even know him."

I looked up from my mound of pancake cement. "His name's Patrick, and he's a really great guy," I said.

"Then why haven't we met him, if he's so wonderful?" my father asked.

I shrugged. I didn't tell him I was afraid they wouldn't like him, that he had long hair. My father hated seeing boys with long hair, called them hippies in a derisive tone. "*He looks like a girl,*" he'd grumble.

And then there was Patrick's black leather jacket and his chains. Strike one, strike two, strike three.

I wanted them to know what a good person he was, how responsible. I should have told them he had a job but instead I said, "We used a condom."

"Well, *that's* comforting," my father said. He walked into the living room and back again, hands in his pockets. "I'm very disappointed in you, Libby."

"You don't understand," I said. "We love each other."

Where had that come from? The look on my mother's face reflected the surprise I felt after the words escaped my mouth, but I hated that they were thinking about me in bed with Patrick, thinking I was a tramp. It was humiliating. I just wanted to flee from the kitchen and the mound of pancakes and the looks on their faces.

I'd had to call the Bradshaws and apologize, and offer to buy them a new bedspread and sheets (which they kindly declined). I was grounded for a month.

"You will come right home after school and you will not go out on Saturday nights for a month except to work," my father had said. "I don't ever want to see you with that boy."

Of course we saw each other at school every day. For the month I was grounded Patrick picked me up at the bus stop in the morning and dropped me there after school. After the month was over, when I could go out again in the evenings and weekends, I spent all my time with him. My parents knew who I was with but they never asked and I never said. I'm sure they breathed an enormous sigh of relief the day I left for college, mostly grateful that I hadn't gotten knocked up.

Five

─❧ ❦ ❧─

Michael called later in the day to say he'd have to meet me at my parents' house, that his meeting was running long.

"Should I bring anything?" he asked.

"No, I've got some wine. We're good. Listen, Michael . . . do you have a second or are you in a hurry?" I wanted to plant a seed about not getting married.

"I've got to run," he said. "George is waiting for me."

I sat for a moment after he hung up, thinking I should at least have told him not to say anything to my parents about our getting engaged. Well, I could catch him later.

Rufus was asleep on my bed, looking like a big ball of gray flannel. He opened one eye when he heard me open the closet door. He yawned and stretched and then walked over to the edge of the bed, where he stood meowing, ready to weigh in on what I was going to wear. My clothes hung neatly: jeans on one side, casual pants next, dress pants after that. Blouses, then dressy tops, then casual tops, then skirts and a few dresses. In one corner were the things Michael left at my house: a few pairs of khakis, two pairs of jeans and four shirts. The closet was tidy and organized. Kind of like my life.

While I grabbed a pair of jeans Rufus continued to meow, and as I pulled them on he extended a paw toward me, waving me over. It was his game. He liked attention. "Pet me," he'd say if he could talk. "Just a little scratch around the ears." So I did.

I put on a sleeveless gold V-neck top, a wide leather belt and black boots, and pulled out a jacket with a black and tan pattern. Not bad for an old broad, I thought.

I was on my way to the bathroom to check my makeup and hair when I thought to look at my e-mail to see if Patrick had responded. I didn't expect to hear from him so soon—it had only been a few hours, after all—but a huge smile unfurled on my face when I saw an e-mail with an unfamiliar screen name, KayakDude, and the subject line *Re: Your past comes back to haunt you.* I laughed out loud, feeling as if I'd just been invited to the prom. My heart thumped as I opened the e-mail.

> **Libby,**
> **Wow! You brightened my day. It's great to hear from you, and no, of course I haven't forgotten you. How could I?**

I smiled.

> **I've often wondered where you were and how you were doing. I looked for your name when I first joined Search-ForSchoolmates.com and hoped someday I'd find it. And here you are!**
> **So, okay, here's my life in a nutshell: I was married, then divorced, and I have a son who's almost 30. He's married and has two little ones. It's amazing being a grandpa. Do you have kids? Are you a grandma? Man, that's a concept.**

You heard right—I did move to Florida and I'm still here in a small town on the Gulf Coast. Like the rest of Florida it's growing fast but we still have miles of undeveloped sugar-white sand beaches. I have a sea-kayak tour business that I run in tourist season, plus I own a couple of apartment buildings that keep me pretty busy, always something to fix or rehab. Or a deadbeat tenant. But mostly I enjoy it. I've had a great life.

Yeah, that New Year's Eve is one of my favorite memories, too. Man, I'm flashing back now and remembering when Jack Bradshaw's folks came home early. Whew, that was embarrassing, wasn't it? I'd forgotten that part until just now. Jack's mom was pretty freaked out, wasn't she? I'm sort of remembering that you got in big trouble over it, too, but can't remember how.

Do you keep in touch with anyone from high school? I haven't been to Chicago in years and years. My parents moved to Florida not long after I did and my brothers went out west so I lost track of everyone. Do you ever hear anything about Sophie? Pete?

So glad you e-mailed me! I'm not so great at this e-mail thing (never took typing in high school—who knew guys would need something like that?) but I look forward to hearing from you again. Tell me all about your life.

Peace,

Patrick

P.S. Worth the fifty bucks! Check's in the mail.

Peace. That sounded so much like him. The sea-kayaking business sounded exactly right, too. No corporate crap for Patrick Harrison. I laughed. I had an image of him sitting at his computer, typing with two fingers, a cigarette hanging out of his mouth, long hair in a ponytail. It was silly, really, how happy I was that he remembered me; like a kid with a new best friend. I could see his face clearly—his dark eyes and sweet smile. What did he look like now? Did he still have long hair? Did he have hair at all? Was he still cute? And what would "cute" mean at fifty?

Sophie would freak out. I wanted to answer the e-mail right that second, but only had time to read it over once more before I had to finish getting dressed.

I checked my eye shadow, added a little more blush and brushed my hair, and tried to see myself with Patrick's eyes. What would he see? A reasonably attractive fifty-year-old woman with gray strands in her curly brown hair. Too much gray? Did it make me look old? Would he recognize me after thirty years? I thought I looked decent, but what did I really know? How can you be objective about the face you've been looking at every day for fifty years?

∿

Michael's car was already in the driveway when I pulled up to my parents' house, which totally pissed me off. Why hadn't he called to pick me up if he was going to make it early? How long had he been there and what was he talking about? He'd better not have said anything about our engagement. I would lose it if he had. I could imagine hitting him over the head with my purse. (Not that I'm a hitter.) I didn't really think he'd say anything without me, but Michael was unpredictable these days and I was irritated by the possibility. My sister's car was there as well and I prayed the whole damned family wouldn't be exclaiming over the big news when I walked in.

The living room was empty, but tidy as usual, with bowls

of pistachios on the mahogany end tables, magazines stacked neatly on the coffee table.

"Where is everybody?" I yelled.

"In here," my mother called from the back of the house. As I walked down the short hallway I heard whispering sounds and someone saying, "Shhhh."

Goddamn it, I thought, he's told them. I was furious when I turned the corner, thinking what the hell I'd say, ready to deny everything, but then I was assaulted by shouts of "Surprise!" as twenty or thirty people stood among black balloons (it wasn't until later I'd notice they were emblazoned with 50 or OVER THE HILL) and black streamers strung across the kitchen.

A fucking surprise party.

I'd made Michael swear more than once that he'd never do this and yet there was his face, right smack-dab in front, with a big, satisfied smile.

I wanted to smack him.

Six

—◌ 🟊 ◌—

S orry," Sophie said, looking sheepish. "I told him not to do it, I swear." Pete handed me a large vodka on the rocks with two olives and said, "Drink up. You'll be fine."

My sister, Jill, raised a glass. "Happy birthday," she toasted. "You know, I didn't like it when you went off to kindergarten without me or when you got to wear panty hose first or go to a movie with a boy, but now for the first time in my life I'm glad you're the oldest." She looked beautiful (and young) in a low-cut wraparound dress and heels. Her husband, Mark, wore a bright white shirt and sport coat, and even Jason, their eighteen-year-old, was dressed up (for him) in a V-neck sweater and unripped jeans. They looked like they'd just walked off the pages of a J.Crew catalog.

Jill was the solid, responsible, dependable one. The anti-Libby. She and Mark had been high school sweethearts, had been married now for twenty-eight years and had three beautiful, well-adjusted children who considered Jill and Mark friends as well as parents. Two of their kids were married and lived out of town, and they had four grandchildren who were, of course, smart and adorable.

Behind Jill was my favorite client, Mrs. Rosatti, resplendent in one of her signature outfits: purple pants with a purple and red jacket that had epaulettes on the shoulders, and large gold buttons.

How long had Michael been planning this? Had he gone through my address book? And when did he begin thinking a surprise party was a good idea? Before or after he promised never to do it?

People were lined up as if to pay their respects; they hugged me, patted me on the back and wished me a happy fiftieth birthday, the birthday I'd hoped would pass quickly and quietly. It felt like a funeral.

"Were you surprised?" my mom asked. Apparently she hadn't noticed the shock (or revulsion) on my face when I walked in.

"Completely," I said.

A smile filled her face. "Oh, *good*," she said. "I was so worried I would spill the beans."

Didn't *anybody* know how much I hated surprise parties?

My dad wrapped me in a big bear hug. "Happy birthday, pumpkin. Hard to believe you're fifty. Seems like just yesterday I was teaching you to use a power saw." Strands of white hair made a valiant effort to cover his scalp. His blue eyes sparkled.

I laughed. "Daddy's little tomboy." He and I shared a love of building things, of fixing things and figuring them out.

"You don't look a day over twenty," he said.

"You're prejudiced," I said.

"You're right. Truth is, you don't look a day over thirty." I laughed and kissed his soft cheek. My father was eighty-two but looked no older than seventy. He was tall and thin and had an energetic glow about him. He walked every morning and played golf whenever he could, spurning the use of carts.

My mother hadn't made any of my favorite foods as her
e-mail had promised; she'd ordered them: baby back ribs,
jalapeño corn bread, potato salad, corn on the cob. I'm sure
it was good food—everyone seemed to enjoy it—but I didn't
have much of an appetite. I drank a lot of vodka, though.

Beatrice Rosatti, my client, brought me a plate when I
flopped down on the couch, the first time I'd sat all evening.
Bea was a retired kindergarten teacher. She'd been married
for forty-nine years when, five years earlier, her husband
died in his sleep as he lay next to her. She'd hinted that
he'd died while they were having sex, but I didn't pursue the
subject.

Now she had a boyfriend named Dominick whom she'd
met online.

"You look like you need nourishment," she said, unfold-
ing a napkin on my lap. "Happy birthday, darlin'. Are you
enjoying your party?" Her platinum blond hair was pulled
up in a complicated froth about her head with rhinestone
clips strategically placed.

"Sure," I said, picking at a rib. She raised a finely pen-
ciled eyebrow. Something in my tone, I suppose.

"Were you surprised?"

"That's an understatement," I said. "I told Michael about
a billion times that I hate surprise parties and never wanted
him to throw one for me." There's truth in too much vodka.

"Oh my," Bea said. Dominick came up and handed her a
glass of wine. He leaned over and kissed my cheek. "Happy
birthday, dear girl. Having a good time?"

Bea and I looked at each other. She raised that eyebrow
again and we burst out laughing. Dominick looked puzzled.
"I'll never understand women," he said. "And I'm too old to
start now." He was eighty-seven to Bea's eighty.

"Seems we'll have something important to talk about

this week," she said. "You're coming over, right? I have a lot of work for you."

"Right," I said. "We'll talk."

⋎

My mother had made carrot cake with cream cheese frosting. My favorite. It blazed with fifty candles.

"Somebody get a fire extinguisher," I said.

Everyone sang "Happy Birthday," a few actually on key, and I blew out the candles before the house could catch fire. Michael poured champagne.

We hadn't spoken much during the evening; there'd been too many people, too much tumult, and Michael had been busy playing host, the guy who'd pulled off the impossible. I wasn't sure I liked this new, stealth Michael.

Once everyone had a glass he whistled loudly to get their attention, a piercing sound that caused people to wince. "A toast to the birthday girl," he said when it was quiet, holding up his glass. "To the best-looking fifty-year-old I know." Shouts of "Here, here!" I think I blushed. Or maybe it was just a hot flash. "To the love of my life," Michael continued, clinking his glass to mine, and we all took a sip.

But Michael wasn't finished.

He whistled again, that same shrill sound. Everyone watched expectantly while my heart sank to my stomach, and before I had time to figure out how to head this off, he raised his glass again and said, "To my future wife."

Confused silence.

Then Michael practically shouted, "I proposed last night and Libby said yes!"

I thought I was going to throw up.

My Aunt Shirley let out a squeal. Uncle Charlie came over and thumped Michael on the back. Faces loomed before me like balloons, many with expressions of surprise, others with wide grins, the tinkling of glasses touching in the air. Another wave of hugs and kisses and now "Congratulations," and "It's about time." I could hardly breathe.

Sophie watched me carefully, hoping, I suppose, that I wouldn't do or say something I'd regret. Her daughters, Tiffany and Danielle, gathered around, jumping up and down, begging to be bridesmaids, suggesting colors for the dresses. Ironically it was for Danielle's wedding that I was making those unfortunate purple creations with the ruffles, all shiny with bows at the sweetheart necklines. And still I stood there, thinking we could simply use those same dresses. That's what I was thinking. As if I would even have a wedding with bridesmaids. As if, even if I did, I would make anyone wear a dress like that. Clearly my mind had gone missing and I was operating in a haze of stupidity. And vodka.

If I could whistle like Michael, I thought, I'd do it and then I'd tell them all it was a cruel joke, that Michael and I were not getting married. But I couldn't whistle. I could barely speak. What a mess. My whole family, all my friends, Michael's parents, my favorite client, all thought I was engaged.

And they were all so damned happy.

Seven

—◦❦◦—

And then they were all gone, the house empty of everyone except me, Michael, his parents and mine. One big, happy family.

"I'm thrilled about your news," my mother said. "Welcome to the family, Michael." She kissed him and he smiled broadly.

"What kind of wedding are you going to have?" Michael's mother asked.

"A small one," he said at the same time I said, "We haven't gotten that far."

Jeez, did he already have the damn thing planned out?

"I'm very happy for you, honey." This from my father. He put his arm around me and pulled me close. "Now I can stop worrying about you."

"Why would you worry about me?"

"You're my daughter. It's in my job description."

"I'm your *middle-aged* daughter."

"You're still my little girl." His blue eyes shone with tenderness and I hugged him tightly.

"And my new daughter," Michael's father said.

Michael beamed.

"Okay, well, time to go." Let's end on a high note, I thought.

We walked outside and Michael helped his parents into his car. I wanted to tell him to go home after he dropped them off, to his own house, but I knew he'd be coming to mine. His *fiancée's* house.

ᴠ

I was pouring a couple glasses of wine when Michael walked in. He put his arms around me from behind. "My parents are so happy." I gave him a glass. "We should have champagne," he said.

He was thinking celebration.

I was thinking fortification.

"Let's go sit in the living room," I said. Michael brought the bottle. I sat in the wingback chair near the fireplace and Rufus jumped in my lap and curled up into a fat, woolly ball. Michael sat on the couch and patted the seat beside him.

"Come sit here," he said.

"We need to talk."

"I know, but can't we do it side by side? Come sit with me." He was completely oblivious to the fact that I was about to stick a pin in his bubble of joy.

"Things are moving a little fast for me, Michael." He paused, wineglass in midair, eyes searching mine. Rufus looked up at me and then at Michael. I scratched his neck. Michael drained his wine, then poured himself more.

"Fast?" he said. "You think two years is fast?"

"It's not about how long we've been together, it's about a couple of things. For one, it's how you sprang this proposal on me in the restaurant in front of all those people in spite of the fact that you knew I didn't want to get married again."

"I took a chance that after two years you might have

changed your mind. And apparently you had. You said yes, Libby."

I hadn't exactly said yes, but I knew I wouldn't get anywhere with that argument. "I know, I'm sorry, but I felt pressured." He sucked on the inside of his cheek. "And then you make a big announcement in front of our family and friends before I'm even used to the idea." I was getting riled up now. On a roll. "And you threw me a *surprise party* even though you promised me, *swore* to me, you never would." Rufus jumped off my lap. I hated the words coming out of my mouth. When said aloud they seemed ridiculous, just plain ungrateful. Most women would love the kind of surprises Michael had planned for me.

"I love you. I wanted to do something special for you. Is that so terrible?"

"It's not that it's terrible. It's that you didn't think about how all this might affect me."

"I did, Libby. I thought about it a lot. I thought it would make you happy. I thought when you said yes, you wanted to marry me, that you meant it. So I figured you'd be excited to tell everyone and, okay, maybe I got carried away with my happiness and so I just said it." He leaned forward. "I'm sorry I didn't clear it with you first. I'm sorry if that's not how you wanted to do it. I really am." I felt deflated. Stupid. Petty. "And I'm sorry you hated the surprise party."

He looked sad, and sincerely apologetic. "I didn't *hate* the surprise party."

"Everyone always says they don't want a surprise party, but nobody means it. I really didn't think you meant it. I thought you'd have a great time with all your friends and family around."

I was suddenly exhausted. Every time Michael opened his mouth I felt worse and worse. His intentions had been so

good and all I could do was complain about it all. My indig-
nation was in a puddle at my feet and in its place was a big
pool of guilt.

"I love you, Libby, and I'm so happy we're engaged." *All
right,* I wanted to scream. *Enough!*

"I love you, too. I think I'm overtired. Too much excitement for the last couple of days." He smiled. "Let's just go to
bed and sort this all out tomorrow, okay?"

"You're not mad?"

"I'm not mad."

Was I?

Should I be?

It didn't matter. I had no energy left for anger. We took
the wine into the kitchen.

"Let's have one more toast before we go to bed," Michael
said, pouring a splash into each glass.

Was he serious? "Michael, really, I'm exhausted."

"Just a little toast to our life together."

It felt as if bees were buzzing around my head. "Have
you heard a word I've said?" Michael flinched. "I've had
enough wine!" He looked at the bottle on the counter. "I'm
overwhelmed, Michael. I've had enough toasts to last a lifetime and I am going to bed now."

I left him there in the kitchen with a wineglass in his
hand and an expression of pure confusion on his face. And I
thought, What is he, stupid?

Eight

◦─᳐◦

Michael got out of bed very early in the morning and I pretended to be asleep. He dressed quietly, kissed me gently on the cheek—I didn't move—and left to play racquetball. When I heard the front door close behind him I sighed. I wouldn't see him again until Tuesday or Wednesday since we rarely spent Sunday nights together.

Rufus came to take Michael's place, curling up against my side, draping a paw on my hip. I hadn't slept well but as soon as Rufus and I were alone I fell into a comalike slumber. Later, after I made a small pot of French roast and buttered a toasted English muffin, I took my breakfast to my desk and turned on my computer. I reread Patrick's e-mail and felt happy all over again. I was excited to answer it but first I wrote an e-mail to Sophie:

What are Michael and I doing getting engaged? What are we, *twelve*? He's almost sixty, for chrissakes. Next thing you know, I'll be having bridal showers and registering for china. Can you just see Michael and me running through Crate & Barrel with one of those scanner

guns? What the hell would we even scan? It's not as if I don't already have china and crystal and fondue pots and lava lamps from my first two weddings.

And that surprise party and the big announcement . . . kill me now.

The phone rang within ten minutes, as I knew it would. Sophie was always connected. I usually gave her a hard time about how excessive and annoying that was, especially when we were having lunch or shopping and she was checking her iPhone every other minute, but I loved it when I needed her.

"The party was fun," she said. "Even you looked like you were having a good time."

"Once I got over my initial irritation it was tolerable," I said. "But I don't understand why he did it, knowing how I feel about surprise parties."

"I really did try to talk him out of it."

"I'm sure you did. Thing is, I was feeling okay about it, making an effort to enjoy it even though I see no reason to celebrate turning fifty, and then he made that birthday toast and that was fine, and then he whistled and I knew what he was going to do and there was no way to stop him and I just felt sick."

"I know. But he didn't know how you were feeling, did he?"

"No. I didn't have a chance to talk to him."

"Well, so it's done and everyone knows. Maybe you should stop concentrating on what he did and really consider what you want. Think about how nice your life's been the last couple of years with Michael."

"I know. I have thought about that."

"It's been peaceful. It's been companionable. You enjoy the same things, you travel, you like each other's families. Michael's a man you can grow old with."

"God, you're like president of his fan club."

"Well, he's good for you, Libby. I just don't want you to do anything you'll regret. Take a deep breath," she said. "Slow down. Give yourself some time to get used to the idea."

"Hey," I said, tired of thinking about Michael. "Remember Patrick Harrison?"

Of course she did. I told her how we'd hooked up and about our e-mails. "God, Patrick Harrison. That was a hundred years ago."

"I know."

"Libby," Sophie said, "is that what this is all about, with Michael?"

"No, of course not," I said. "It has nothing to do with Michael."

"Are you sure?"

"I am, Sophie. Do you think I would chuck everything because I exchanged e-mails with my high school boyfriend? First of all, he lives in Florida. Secondly, I haven't seen him in thirty-some years. Plus, he wasn't my type back then, what would make him my type now?"

"What do you mean he wasn't your type? You were crazy about him."

"I know, but it didn't last, did it? He was a hood. I was preppy. He majored in vocational ed. I was on the college track."

"Opposites attract."

"Only until I went off to college," I reminded her. "And then there's the minor detail that I have a life with Michael, and even if I don't want to marry him, I like our life together."

"So, tell me about your e-mails," Sophie said.

She was pleased that Patrick had asked about her and Pete. Laughed that he was a grandfather. Loved his sea-kayaking business.

"I wonder what he looks like," she said. "He was really cute thirty years ago."

"Probably fat and bald now," I said.

"I bet not," she said, and I could hear the smile in her voice.

❧

Patrick, I wrote after Sophie and I had hung up.

It was so great to hear from you. Isn't this amazing? Who would think we'd be in touch again after all these years?

You, a grandfather—how is that possible? How did we get to be so old? No, I'm not a grandmother, never had children. I've been married twice (divorced now) but children weren't part of the picture(s). I wish they had been but life doesn't always turn out the way you expect, does it?

The sea-kayaking business seems so much like something you'd do. I knew you wouldn't be an accountant or lawyer or some other "establishment" dude. Kayak Dude—perfect.

Yes, Jack Bradshaw's parents came home when we were in their bedroom—a very humiliating experience. Especially since they were good friends with my parents, who they called first thing the next morning. What a scene at my house that day! I think I was grounded for a year after that. But, as I recall, we still managed to see each other.

Sophie and Pete got married and still are. Isn't that great? They have two gorgeous daughters, one who's getting married soon. I'm a dress designer/seamstress and I'm making the bridesmaid dresses for the wed-

ding. Tiffany, their youngest (15), is coming in for a fitting today. She looks just like Sophie did at that age, except she's got lots of piercings and spiky hair—Sophie with an edge. They're a fabulous family. In fact I just got off the phone with Sophie and she says hi!

As for my life, it's been wonderful. Okay, yeah, I've been married and divorced twice but I consider that character building. Now I have a significant other and we've been together almost two years. The other night he asked me to marry him and I have to say it shocked the hell out of me. I never thought I'd get married again, but how could I say no to a three-carat diamond?

Libby

Nine

—◦ ❦ ◦—

Tiffany pivoted slowly as I pinned the hem of her purple bridesmaid dress.

"I'm going to walk down the aisle in front of two hundred people looking like an iris on steroids," she said, scrunching up her nose. "This is totally gross."

"You're going to look beautiful no matter what you're wearing," I told her. "Think of it as wardrobe. Imagine you're an actress or a rock star and you're doing a personal appearance, and just walk down that aisle like a queen. Like you're Cher or Madonna or someone."

"Oh my god, they're so old. How about Katy Perry?" she said. "Just do a big cutout here in the middle so my belly button shows, rip off these stupid sleeves and lower the neckline. What do you think?"

Tiffany's hair, which used to be blond, was a shade of red found most often on traffic signals. It clashed madly with the purple dress. She had a piercing through her eyebrow where she wore a small silver ring, four piercings in her left ear and two in her right. She had a tongue piercing as well, which glinted silver when she talked. It amazed me that Sophie was so nonchalant about all this body maiming. "All those holes will close," she'd say. "At least she's not into tattoos."

"Not yet," I'd say.

Now Tiffany asked, "So when are you guys getting married?"

"I don't know."

"Are you going to have a big wedding?"

"No, I'm too old for that," I said. "Besides, I've been married twice already. How many weddings does one person need?"

She giggled. "I think you should have a big wedding. I want to be a bridesmaid."

"I'd make you wear a dress just like this," I said, fluffing her big purple sleeve, "only in lime green. What do you think about that?"

She pointed her finger into her mouth and made a gagging sound.

"Turn," I told her and finished pinning the hem.

"I'm going to the movies later with Ryan," she said as I helped her out of the dress and she pulled her jeans on.

"Who's Ryan?"

"Christopher's brother." Christopher was the groom. "I'll be walking down the aisle with him."

"Aren't you a little young to date?" I said, sounding like an old lady. It seemed like last week I was taking her and Danielle to Kiddieland.

"I'm *fifteen*."

"Well, fun," I said, hoping they'd still like each other by the time the wedding got here, and then realizing how cynical that was.

"He's hot," she said, and blushed. Her smile was shy and her eyes shone. Young love, I thought enviously. I remembered those days.

"So how do you know when you're in love?" she asked. As if I knew.

"Oh honey, you're not in love. You just met him."

"So?" she said, indignant. "Haven't you heard of love at first sight?"

"Sure, in books. In real life it's called lust." What was wrong with me? Was I really saying this to a fifteen-year-old? Fortunately, I resisted giving her the wisdom of my many failed relationships: that Ryan was only the first in a line of men who would break her heart and underachieve her expectations. "Sorry, sweetie. I didn't mean that. It happens. Just not often. And when it does you just know it," I said. "But being in love at fifteen is different from being in love at fifty."

"Different how?"

"Oh man, where to begin," I said. I started steaming the hem and Tiffany flopped down into the big chair, looking quickly at her iPhone but then amazingly putting it down.

"Were you in love at fifteen?" she asked.

"No. The first time I fell in love I was seventeen."

"Was it love at first sight?"

I had to laugh. "It kind of was," I admitted. "I met him at a party and when he walked in the door my heart started pounding."

"Oh god, that's what happened to me!" Tiffany squealed, her face lighting up like neon.

"It's a wonderful feeling. And when you're young you think nothing will ever change that. You think it'll last forever."

"Sometimes it does," Tiffany said. "Look at my mom and dad."

"Touché."

"What happened to you and your guy?"

"I went away to college and we lost touch," I said.

She raised her eyebrows and the little silver hoop caught the light. "Just like that?" she said.

"Well, it didn't happen overnight. At first I was really depressed being away from him and I just wanted to go home. I thought going off to college had been a huge mistake and I wanted to quit school and go home and marry him."

"He asked you to *marry* him?"

"Well . . . no," I admitted. "It was just my fantasy. In fact, he was the one who convinced me to stay in school. He said he wasn't going anywhere and that I just needed time to get used to it. He said I was really lucky to have the opportunity and it was going to be important for my future, for our future together." I hadn't thought about all of this in years. I had forgotten how encouraging he had been, how adult. At the time I'd worried that he didn't really love me if he could bear to be away from me, but looking at it from my perspective as a fifty-year-old, I realized how selfless and supportive he had been.

"Why didn't he go to college if he was so big on it?"

"His family couldn't afford it. He worked all through high school and then he thought if he worked full-time for another year he could earn enough money to go to college after that."

I spread out the dress on the worktable, pulled up a high stool and started hand-stitching the hem.

"So what happened to you two? Why didn't you stay together? He sounds like a cool guy."

"He *was* a cool guy." I thought about his e-mail, how happy he'd been to hear from me. *Peace,* he had said. "When I first got to school we called each other all the time and missed each other desperately and I just lived for Christmas break, and then when I got home we were so happy to be together. But it was a little bit awkward, too. We were living

different lives and didn't have that much in common anymore. He was working at a discount store; I was worried
about exams. He was still living at home; I was on my own,
I'd started to make friends at school—you know, that kind of
thing. It just wasn't quite the same."

"How sad."

"Oh well, things happen," I said.

"So how was it different when you fell in love with Michael?"

Let me count the ways.

"It's hard to explain," I said. "Maybe we can save that
conversation for another time. Right now I've got to gather
up some stuff to take to a client." I didn't, I just didn't want
to get into all of that. I thought it best to keep my cynical
mouth shut. Let her have her dreams now. They'd be dashed
soon enough.

Tiffany grabbed her phone, kissed me and left, thumbs
flying on the Lilliputian keyboard.

I finished hemming her dress and picked up another. I
wanted to complete all four and deliver them. I was going
blind with all that purple.

Later I checked my e-mail. It wasn't until I saw the message from Patrick that I realized I'd been holding my breath.

Libby,
    **You've been married twice and getting ready to do
it again? Wow, either you're a glutton for punishment
or an eternal optimist. Seriously, tho, congratulations.
Yeah, I guess three carats can be pretty persuasive.**
    **I came close a second time but got cold feet before
we made it to the altar. I guess it wasn't so much getting married that scared me as that she was great but
not someone I thought I'd want to spend my life with.**

Do you have a picture? I'm attaching one of me with my son's family taken last summer when I visited them. Now, before you open it remember that I am 32 years older and almost that many pounds bigger than I was the last time you saw me. So be kind. The heart's the same but the body sure isn't.

Hey, can I call you sometime? It'd sure be easier than typing, wouldn't it? And it'd be great to hear your voice. Here's my number if you want to call me: 850-555-6768.

Patrick

Call? Like on the phone? Stupidly, that hadn't occurred to me. It was as if he only existed in the virtual world. Now, realizing I could actually talk to him, I was unnerved. It was one thing to write; you could think about what to say before saying it. But talk? That depended on a mutual chemistry, didn't it? A connection. What if we didn't have that? What if we had nothing to say to each other? I liked this little fantasy we had going. Why ruin it?

But I was dying to see what he looked like. No harm in downloading the photo.

And there he was.

I studied the current-day Patrick for several minutes, squinting to reveal the face I had known. It took some getting used to but he was there, familiar and not, all at the same time. I laughed out loud. Patrick had aged well. *He was cute!* Yes, he was heavier, his face was fuller than I remembered, but he wasn't fat. And he wasn't bald. His hair was salt and pepper, mostly pepper, but it seemed as thick as ever and was longish, wavy, brushing his collar. He and his son sat on a porch step, leaning toward each other with big matching grins. Two young boys and a pretty dark-haired woman sat on the step below them laughing at the camera, as if someone had just told a great joke. There were laugh lines around Patrick's eyes and mouth. He wore jeans and a T-shirt with the sleeves rolled up and a cigarette in his hand. He still smokes, I thought. I had forgotten how much we both smoked back then.

He looked solid and weathered and ruggedly handsome. I thought if I saw him on the street today I would turn to study him appreciatively. He didn't look like the boy I'd known, but he'd turned into a fine-looking man.

I wrote his phone number on a Post-it thinking I might call him that evening, and took it with me to the kitchen to make myself some dinner.

❧

I felt lighthearted as I put together a chopped salad with Bibb lettuce, arugula, spinach, hard-boiled eggs, red onion, artichoke hearts, raisins and sunflower seeds. I had a sense of anticipation as I thought about Patrick's e-mail and his picture. The familiarity of him felt good and comfortable.

I was checking a loaf of Asiago cheese bread warming in the oven when I heard a key in the front door. My heart skipped a beat and the oven door slammed shut before I re-alized it wasn't a burglar, it was Michael. The fear dissolved and was replaced with exasperation. What the fuck was he doing here now?

"Lib," he called.

"In here," I said and heard him drop keys on the table by the front door. Something else dropped as well, probably an overnight bag, and the sound made me furious.

"Mmmm, looks good," he said, kissing me.

"What are you doing here?"

He looked startled. "Nice welcome for your fiancé," he said.

Fiancé.

"You never come over on Sunday night. You could have at least called."

"I did. I left you a message."

I hadn't checked my messages all day. I looked over at the answering machine—a big red 1 blinked at me.

"Well, so what's the occasion?" I asked, making an effort to keep my tone even.

"I just wanted to spend the evening with you. I think we should get used to spending more time together, don't you?"

"Michael, you can't just change things because you think we should. We need to talk about it together, make decisions together. I have things to do tonight. I have work to do. I wasn't planning on you being here."

"Well, shit, Lib, you can do your work," he said. "I don't expect us to be together every second. When we're married we're going to have our own things to do."

Thank god for that, I thought. I pulled the bread out of the oven and clattered the baking pan on the counter.

"Tonight doesn't work for me," I said.

"I'll just sit in the living room and watch TV. You won't even know I'm here."

"I'll know you're here," I said, louder than I meant to. "It doesn't work for me, Michael."

He studied me. "So what you're saying is you want me to go home, is that it?"

"*Yes!*"

Silence. Michael pursed his lips. He looked out the window, jiggled the change in his pocket. "Fine," he said and turned to go. But then he paused in front of the Post-it on the counter. "Who's Patrick?" he asked, turning around, thrusting it toward me.

Oh shit. "No one," I said. "A friend."

"A friend?" he said. "I've never heard you mention anyone named Patrick."

So what? I wanted to shout. He put a ring on my finger and now I had no life of my own? I had to divulge every aspect of my life, every thought, every person I talked to? But I took a breath and contained myself, kept my voice even.

"He's someone I knew in high school. He lives in Florida. He got in touch with me and we've e-mailed a couple of times."

"How'd he get in touch with you?"

"Oh for Christ's sake, what's with the interrogation?" Michael's eyes flashed. "He found me on SearchForSchoolmates .com," I said. "You know, that website where you find people from high school."

"When did he do that?"

"All right, that's enough with the twenty questions. You're making a big deal out of nothing."

Michael's gaze bore into me, making me feel guilty, as if I'd done something horrible.

"Jesus, Libby," he said, taking off his glasses and rubbing the bridge of his nose. "It doesn't feel like nothing to me. It feels a little coincidental, actually, that you've been e-mailing some guy from high school and now you're having second thoughts about our engagement. Does that strike you as odd? Because it does me. What would you think if you were me?" He looked at me, challenging me to dispute this. I could see how it looked to him: deceitful and sneaky. But right then I didn't care.

"You're blowing this up out of proportion, Michael. One has nothing to do with the other."

"Then why don't you just explain one and then the other," he said and sat down at the table, arms folded across his chest. "Well?"

I bristled. "Well what?" All I needed was a spotlight shining down on me to complete the atmosphere.

"Tell me about this Patrick person. Tell me what's going on with him. Tell me what's going on with us. Tell me why it was so terrible that I announced our engagement. Tell me why you're upset that I came over today. Take your pick of topics."

"I don't appreciate your tone, Michael." He sat quietly, staring. "Nothing's going on with Patrick. Nothing. He's someone I knew in high school who got in touch with me." All right, so I got in touch with him, but I wasn't moved to set that record straight. "We've e-mailed a few times. End of story."

Of course, it wasn't the end of the story; it was just the beginning. But at that time I didn't really think there would be much more to tell, and I did think that Michael was overreacting. Yes, I was stirring up feelings, but they were *ancient* feelings. And it wasn't so much about Patrick as it was about me and how much I missed that kind of intensity and passion. It was exactly what Tiffany and I had talked about.

"Okay, so what's going on with us?" he said.

"I don't know." Not the right answer, I knew.

Michael shook his head and looked at his hands. "Are we engaged or not?"

"I don't know."

His face darkened. His eyes flashed. I thought he was going to pick up something and throw it (nothing dangerous; that wouldn't be Michael), but then he just slumped forward. "What do you mean, you don't know? Either we are or we're not."

"You've been making all these decisions about us as if you're the only one in this relationship. I feel out of control, Michael. You decide we're going to get married. You decide when it's time to tell everyone. You decide we need to spend more time together. These are life-changing decisions. These are things we should decide together."

He got up and got a glass of water, drank it down and set the glass in the sink with a loud thunk. He stood at the sink, his back rigid.

"Maybe you need a break from me," he said, turning around. He ran his hand over his head.

A *break*? Oh my god, I practically swooned with the relief that would bring. But I didn't want to appear eager. "What do you mean?" I said.

"Maybe you need time to figure out what you want, if you want to marry me. Decide if you want your e-mail boyfriend or me."

"Oh, Michael."

"What? What am I supposed to think, Libby? It feels like you're hiding something and I don't like it. I don't like any of it."

"I'm not hiding anything." Was I?

"Maybe, maybe not. But something's going on with you and I don't know what it is. I don't even know how you feel about me anymore."

"I don't know how I feel about anything."

"Great."

"It's all just overwhelming to me, Michael. Can you try to understand that, to see it from my point of view?" He apparently thought that was a rhetorical question. "I'm sorry," I said. "I know how you must feel but there've been too many decisions made, too many changes."

"I don't know what you want from me, Libby." He turned and walked away. I followed him. He picked up his overnight bag and his keys. "I'm going home," he said. "When you figure out what you want, call me." He opened the door.

What did this mean? "Will I see you Wednesday?"

"No," he said over his shoulder.

"Michael—" I said.

He wheeled around. *"What, Libby? What?* I asked you to marry me and you said yes and now you don't know if you want to anymore. What am I supposed to do with that? I love you but I need to be loved back." I opened my mouth but he put up his hand like a traffic cop. "I'm done for tonight," he said. "I have nothing else to say. I'm going home." And he walked out, shutting the door quietly behind him.

Is there anything that makes you want someone more than when they don't want you? I stood staring at the door feeling weepy and remorseful.

Was he saying if I didn't marry him we were through? Was there no going back? When did marriage become so important to him? I hated the thought of him leaving without giving me the answers to these questions, without knowing what would happen to us, but I couldn't bring myself to run out and stop him. What would I say if I did?

I looked around the house, at the order, the stillness. Was this what I wanted? To live in my perfect little house, alone? I walked from room to room in the solitude, knowing there would be no one there except Rufus, no sounds that Rufus or I did not make.

I ate a few bites of salad and nibbled on some cheese bread, and then cleaned up the kitchen, washing dishes slowly in soapy water instead of putting them in the dishwasher. I dried them and placed them carefully in the cupboard and wiped the countertops until they looked new, moving the offending Post-it as I worked. I straightened the junk drawer, tossing out nails, paper clips and little black rubber things I didn't recognize. Then I went into the living room, straightened the pillows on the sofa and put the newspapers in a basket by the window.

Everything was in its noiseless order. I'd been alone for many years before Michael, and there had been long stretches when there was no man in my life at all, but now that seemed like a lifetime ago. I tried to remember how it had been. Mostly, I thought I'd been happy, enjoying the freedom of being single, not having to consider anyone else in my plans, sitting on the couch eating taco chips and salsa for dinner if I wanted, watching old movies instead of sports. But I could also remember times when I'd sit looking around, unable to read, with nothing on TV, no one to call, and the silence had felt so lonely I'd go to the mall and walk around just to hear some noise and be with people.

I suddenly felt sad and lonely in my house. Was this how it was going to be for the rest of my life? Just me and Rufus in my tidy little bungalow? I'd already been married twice; two failures. If I let Michael go now, what were the chances I'd find someone to share my life with? Hadn't I used up my share of love vouchers?

Ten

—◦❦◦—

After my initial sadness I felt the cool breeze of relief: relief from having to explain myself, relief from making decisions, relief from worrying about Michael's feelings. But I didn't quite know what to do with myself. I flipped through a catalog, watched TV for about four and a half minutes and went for a walk. And then I came back, retrieved the Post-it and studied Patrick's number. I turned it over, flipped it upside down and waved it around as if it were a birthday present I was savoring opening.

Should I?

What if I did and we said a cheery hello, excited to hear each other's voice, and then ran out of conversation in seven seconds and had to suffer through an awkward silence before politely hanging up? Just because things were easy in the virtual world didn't mean they would be easy in reality.

But wasn't it also possible we could have an immediate connection and chat as if we were back in high school? Maybe we would laugh and joke the way we did back then. Maybe it would feel as if no time at all had passed. How fun would that be?

I wondered if Patrick was a different person from the one I knew. Do people change? Every young bride thinks so. Don't we all marry with that bright shining light of what will be? Not what is, but what *will* be once the new hubby gets what it's all about and realizes that sharing his every thought and wish and dream is fun!

Yeah, right.

That's what I'd thought when I married the first time at twenty-two. And the second time at thirty-four. But now at fifty I finally understood: we all like to think we'll change, that we'll be more confident as we grow older, or wiser, more sophisticated, more tolerant, patient, understanding. But deep down we're basically the same people we were when we were fifteen or twenty. And although maybe, with a concerted effort, we can change ourselves, we're never going to change our partner.

So, should I call? Well, it was a fifty-fifty proposition: we'd either connect or we wouldn't. I dialed the number. It rang once and then again as I tapped my fingernail on the desk. Suddenly I got cold feet and was about to slam down the receiver when a voice said, "Hello?" His voice. I recognized it immediately and blood rushed to my face.

"Hello?" he said again.

"Patrick?"

"Yes . . . ?" He paused. "Libby?"

How'd he know?

"Oh, Libby," he exclaimed, "is that you?"

"It is."

"I'm so happy to hear your voice. Man, this is weird, isn't it?" He laughed, a genial, familiar sound, even after thirty-two years. I could see the big smile on his face, but it was the face I last saw thirty-some years ago, not the new one in the picture he'd sent.

"It's very weird. You sound so much like yourself. It takes me back in time."

"Me too," he said. "Little Libby Carson. Wow. Cool. So how are things?"

Unbelievably, I said, "Awful," and as soon as the word was out of my mouth, I wanted to grab it and stuff it right back in. Couldn't I have made a little small talk first?

"What's going on?" he said, his concern reaching like a hug across the wires.

"Michael and I are fighting about this engagement thing. He sort of stormed out earlier."

"Why are you fighting?" he asked.

"I'm not sure I want to get married. It was never in my game plan, so Michael's not very happy with me right now." What possessed me to tell him this? He'd sounded delighted to hear from me, probably thinking this was going to be a lighthearted "remember-when" kind of conversation, and here I was spilling my guts like a kid in confession.

Watch him hang up on me.

"Wow. Well . . . oh man, Libby, I'm sorry," he said. What else could he say? I wished I could take it all back, hang up and start over. Why isn't there a replay button in life? "Are you okay?" he asked.

"I'm okay," I said. "Jeez, I haven't talked to you in thirty-two years and the first thing I do is tell you all my problems."

"It's okay," he said. "I'm not so good with my own problems but I'm dynamite with other people's." I chuckled with the lightness his words brought. "What are you going to do?" he asked.

Appallingly, tears came. I couldn't speak except for small embarrassing mewling sounds.

"Libby?"

"Yes," I said in a high-pitched, whiny, cry-baby voice. It

was so incredibly embarrassing. I was fifty, for god's sake. *Fifty.*

"It'll be okay," Patrick said. "It's hard, but you'll work it out."

"Yeah, I know," I said after regaining a scrap of composure. "I'm sorry to be dumping this on you after all these years, to be crying like a baby—"

"Libby," he interrupted, "don't worry about it, okay? I love other people's misery. It makes me feel superior and I have so few chances to do that." It felt good to laugh. "Look, if you want to talk, I can listen. If you're not comfortable talking to me about it, that's something else, but if you are, then don't worry about it. Talk all you want. We're friends."

"We haven't seen each other in a lifetime."

"Well, so we took a hiatus."

"Tell me about you," I said. "What's going on in your world?" I didn't want to talk anymore. There was no telling what other stupidity could come out of my mouth with little or no provocation.

So Patrick talked and I smiled as I listened to the recognizable cadence of his voice, feeling like I was seventeen again, back in my lavender bedroom with Eric Clapton and David Bowie posters on the walls, idly chattering, making plans to meet before homeroom.

He told me about a kayak tour he'd done the day before. "Most tours take about four hours," he said, "but this one took almost seven. Everything that could go wrong did. There's a name for that, isn't there? What's that called?"

"Murphy's Law," I said.

"I'm renaming it Harrison's Law," he said. "I was already paddling the nine-year-old son when the father got a cramp and decided to walk back, so I had to tow his kayak in. Then when we got back the mom didn't feel well and I'm helping her out of her kayak when she barfs all over it."

I laughed. "At least she didn't barf all over you."

"Really."

"Here I thought you had such a glamorous profession," I said.

"Yes, very glamorous. Cleaning up vomit."

He told me about the weather in Florida and about where he lived on the beach and about his dog named Chewbacca. The sound of his voice was soothing and I was happy just to listen. He told me how his son Ashley was working full-time, putting himself through school, studying filmmaking, and still found time for his wife and two kids. "There's not a big call for filmmakers in South Florida," he said, "but what the hell. It's his life and he'll figure it out. He's a good kid with a good head on his shoulders in spite of the handicap of being raised by me."

What if Patrick and I had stayed together and gotten married? Ashley could have been our son. Surely we wouldn't have named him Ashley, though.

"You must have done something right," I said.

"All I did was enjoy the hell out of raising him."

"How is it that you were the one to raise him?"

"His mom got into drugs when he was little, so I took him. By the time she got it together, he was settled in with me and things were going pretty well, so we left it that way."

"Do they have a good relationship? Your son and his mom?"

"Yeah, now they do. She cleaned up her act after a while. She's doing good now."

"Did she ever try to get custody?"

"No. She moved close, though, and spent as much time

with him as she could. We were friends by that time and we worked it out between us."

"How civilized," I said, thinking of the broken relationships in my wake and the fact that I'd never spoken to any of my exes ever again.

"Yeah, I guess it is. But life's too short to hold grudges."

"God, you're so reasonable. Were you always like that?" I didn't remember this, but we were practically children when we were together. I liked his lightheartedness, his easy optimism. It was so different from what I was used to.

"I guess," he said. "I'm not saying we can control how we feel, but I think we do have choices about how we let what we feel control our lives." He paused. "I should shut up, shouldn't I? I'm sounding like an evangelist."

"Not at all. It's a great attitude. How'd you get to be so mentally healthy?"

"Years of therapy," he said. "Hey, I sent you a photo. Did you get it or are you just ignoring it out of respect for my feelings?"

I laughed. "I did. I love it. Your son looks just like you used to."

"And I don't."

"Well, who does? You look great, though. At least in the picture." He laughed. "And your family's very handsome."

"Send me one of you, okay?"

"I will."

I had a fine, cozy feeling as I hung up, glad I'd called. Patrick's perspective on life made me feel more philosophical about Michael. Maybe a separation would be good for us. Maybe a little distance would help us realize how important our relationship was. "You'll work it out," Patrick had said, and I knew that was true, one way or another. Maybe Michael and I would get married, maybe we wouldn't. Maybe I would end up with Patrick instead. I laughed at this silly fantasy, but imagined seeing him again after all these years, gazing longingly into each other's eyes, devouring each other's face and then hugging excitedly, professing our long-lost love.

Silly stuff. The stuff of romance novels.

I went to my computer and searched through pictures I had stored on my hard drive. There was one from last year's vacation, but I was wearing a blue dress with a large print that made me look like a blimp. What had I been thinking? I made a mental note to get rid of it. There was another photo that wasn't bad but my neck looked saggy. Then I found one taken at a backyard party at Sophie and Pete's. I was lying on the grass, leaning on my elbow as I played with someone's small, blond grandchild. We had both looked up, surprised, when Michael called to me and snapped the picture. Sun glinted off the gray in my hair, making it look like shiny highlights, and I had an open, unself-conscious smile. I was wearing shorts and a low-cut top, and my legs looked long and sleek, even though they're not all that long. Or all that sleek. But the angle was just right.

Patrick,

It was so much fun talking to you. A blast from the past.

So here's a picture. Last time you saw me I wore black eyeliner and had long straightened hair parted down the middle. There are a few other changes as well. Hah! I'm also sending a picture of Sophie and Pete.

Say, didn't you have a big, old black Ford with huge fins that we used to go "parking" in?

Libby

P.S. Do you have a girlfriend?

I couldn't help myself.
A reply came back within minutes.

Girl, the years have treated you well! Are you sure you didn't hire a stand-in?

I laughed out loud.

No, really, you are still beautiful even without the eyeliner.

Thanks for the picture of S & P. It's great to see them! Give me their e-mail addresses, would you? I'd love to contact them.

That was a '61 Ford Starliner, to be specific. I'm flashing back right now. Didn't we used to go to a little covered bridge that was in a housing development somewhere and park there? So neat to pull up these memories.

Peace,

Patrick

P.S. Nope. No girlfriend.

Why did that please me?

Eleven

I didn't call Michael on Monday. I didn't call him on Tues-day. I didn't call him for almost a week. I thought about it, but each time I picked up the phone I decided I wasn't going to be the one to call. Childish, I know. Sometimes it's hard to believe I'm fifty when I do things like that. But if there's one thing I've learned it's that things just don't change all that much as you get older. Inside I feel the way I always did.

I had a boyfriend in fourth grade. His name was Randy Dempsey and he had shiny black hair and a small dark mole beside his right eye. He wore plaid pants and he made me laugh. I passed him a note one day that said

> *I like you.*
> *Do you (____) like me*
> *(____) not like me*
> *(____) love me*

He put an X beside *love me* and that was how I knew he was my boyfriend. Eight is the best time to be in love, when you're young enough to be unself-conscious about your feelings, before you learn about playing games.

That was the last time love felt so uncomplicated and pure. By the time I was in eighth grade, I had a new boyfriend, Jim Evans, and I was rife with confusion. I was shy around boys by then, not knowing what to do or say, and clueless about what was expected of me. And yet Jim asked me to go steady and gave me a gold-colored ring that had an Indian head on it, and I wore it on a chain around my neck. It made me feel supremely secure. But one afternoon we went to the eighth-grade mixer and did the Twist among the crepe-paper streamers and drank punch and talked about everyone at the dance. I went off to the washroom and when I came back, Jim was talking to Kimmie Kramer, she of the blond curls and long eyelashes and multicolored tent dress. They seemed lost in their conversation, heads close together, and I stood watching for a moment while tears formed behind my eyes, and then I turned around and walked out.

I walked home feeling wounded and jealous, thinking that if he wanted to be with Kimmie Kramer, then he could just be with Kimmie Kramer and I would give him back his stupid ring.

For the next couple of days I refused to take Jim's phone calls, and moped around the house making everyone miserable until finally my dad cornered me on the back porch and asked what was wrong.

"Nothing," I said. I didn't want to tell him. He thought I was too young to have a boyfriend and I didn't want him to say anything bad about Jim, even though I was mad at him.

"Something's wrong," my dad said. "Your smile's gone missing. Come on, you can tell your old dad." He put his arm around me, and so I told him my sad story and how betrayed I felt.

"Did you ever ask him what they were talking about?"

"No."

"What if they were talking about how much he likes you?"

I snorted.

"What if they were talking about TV shows? Couldn't they have been talking about"—he searched his brain for one of the shows I liked—"*The Monkees?*"

I shrugged.

"The thing is, pumpkin, you don't know. You just jumped to the conclusion that he likes her better than you. Isn't that right?"

I was starting to get his point.

"I bet that's not true. Put yourself in his place: here you are talking to some boy, just a friend, and Jim sees you and just makes a snap judgment about you and leaves. How would that feel?" I stared at my bony knees and my dad pulled me close. "You're a smart girl, Libby. Just give it some thought. I think you'll see that Jim at least deserves the chance to talk to you. He's been trying, so my guess is he's feeling pretty bad himself right now. He's probably sad that you won't talk to him. Don't you think?"

I nodded into his shoulder. "Well, go call him, honey." This from my dad who didn't want me to have a boyfriend.

And so I did. And my dad was right, of course. Not that they were talking about *The Monkees*, but that Jim had no interest in Kimmie Kramer. Didn't even like her, actually.

And here I was fifty years old, and the feelings, the insecurities, the pride were all the same. When you're young you think being middle-aged means you'll act like an adult. What you don't know until you get here is that in certain things, particularly where love is concerned, we never grow up.

I was ambivalent about my aloneness. But Rufus loved it. He was happy to have me to himself. Especially at bedtime.

He liked to curl up at my side with a paw resting on my hip, and when Michael was there he had to move over to the other side of the bed. He didn't appreciate the displacement. He'd walk around for a while, then stand on me looking at Michael before pawing around in a new spot and settling in. At some point during the night he'd meow and stalk off.

Now he was content.

It seemed odd and empty not to see Michael, not to talk to him. I vacillated between relief and anger, loneliness and tranquility, righteousness and rejection. But I survived. At first I was sad, then I was pissed that he didn't call, that he could just shut down because things hadn't gone his way. Fuck him, I thought. Two could play at that game.

❦

Dominick was at Mrs. Rosatti's when I arrived for our appointment. "Well, here's the engaged lady," he said. Inwardly I rolled my eyes. "Come join us for tea and coffee cake."

Bea looked jazzy in a teal blue pantsuit with splashes of bright white flowers. She wore a chunky white necklace and large hoop earrings. She belonged on Collins Avenue in Miami Beach. Dominick, his shiny bald head fringed with fluffy white hair, was quietly dapper, the antithesis to Bea's in-your-face fashion style. Today he wore a gray cashmere cardigan over a snowy white shirt and navy trousers. This relationship was of the "opposites attract" variety.

Bea put a piece of pastry in front of me and poured me a cup of tea. At first I didn't notice they were hardly speaking to each other, that each of them was addressing their remarks only to me, commenting on the weather, talking about my surprise party. When it finally dawned on me that there was tension in the room I looked up, surprised, first at one, then the other. They were concentrating resolutely on their coffee cake. Bea asked Dominick if he wanted more tea. He said no. She gave him a pointed look and glanced at me.

"Well," he said, suddenly cheerful, "I'd best be on my way. I'll leave you two to your girls' stuff." He kissed Bea on the cheek.

"I'll speak to you later, dear," she said.

"Is everything all right?" I asked when he'd gone.

"Oh yes," she said, clearly lying.

"There was a bit of tension in here."

"Oh, I suppose there was," Bea said. "That was rude. We should have been more discreet with our little tiff."

"You were fine," I said. "What are you 'tiff-ing' about?" I didn't want to think of people in their eighties having a lovers' quarrel. Isn't there a statute of limitations on that kind of bullshit?

"Would you like more tea?" she asked, getting up and lighting the burner under the teakettle. "Or how about a sherry?"

"Nothing, thanks," I said. "Come sit down." She turned off the fire and sat. "So tell me," I said.

"Dominick wants us to move in together and I'm not sure it's a good idea. So he's upset."

"Wow," I said. "It's the same old crap no matter how old you get, isn't it?" She smiled. "Why isn't it a good idea?"

"I've been alone for a long time and I've gotten used to doing things my own way. I don't know that I want to change that. We have such a lovely relationship, but I think part of that is because we don't live together so we don't deal with each other every minute. And at our age, what's the point?"

"What does age have to do with it? You always tell me you're only as old as you feel."

"Ah, throwing my words back in my face, eh?"

"Absolutely. You're using age as an excuse."

"I think I was taken by surprise, if you want to know the truth. It never seemed important to Dominick before, so I just never thought about it."

"Do you think it would work?"

"I suppose I'll have to think about that now, won't I? How are you handling it? You and Michael don't live together and now you're getting married. How do you think that will work?"

"The sixty-four-thousand-dollar question," I said. "I have no idea."

"Sounds like this is the time for the sherry," Bea said and poured two glasses. "So, tell me," she said when she sat.

"Looks like we're sort of in the same boat." I told her everything that had happened, from the proposal to the party to when Michael walked out.

"I don't know Michael well," she said. "He seems like a nice man, but if you're not sure you want to get married, for heaven's sake, don't do it. Make your decision for yourself, not for him."

"I don't want to hurt him."

"Is that a good reason to get married? Sometimes people get hurt when you have different ideas of what you want from a relationship. You can't control that. The only thing you can control is you. If you marry him because you don't want to hurt him, you'll both be sorry."

Simple, logical, sensible advice. She made it sound so easy.

Bea drained her glass and cleared the table. "Come," she said, "let me show you the new clothes I bought, all of which need altering, of course."

"What's the occasion?" I asked, nearly blinded by the array of colors and patterns she displayed before me. There were several summery pants outfits, one with a pattern like an EKG readout in tangerine and green, a pair of electric blue capri pants and a violet evening gown with sequins top to bottom.

"We're going on a cruise to the Caribbean," she said, her eyes sparkling.

"How lovely. Maybe spending so much time together will help you decide if you want to live with him," I said.

"It can't hurt," she said.

"Maybe Michael and I should go with you."

"Come along," Bea said, "you can borrow my clothes!"

Twelve

—☙ ❦ ❧—

Jill was already at the restaurant when I arrived, sitting at a corner table looking elegant and put-together. When Jill was little she was like Pigpen from the *Peanuts* comic strip, clouds of dust always seeming to waft around her. She never wanted to play paper dolls with me (my favorite thing to do when I was a kid, already the little fashionista), but she did it to please me. Jill didn't care about clothes or what she looked like and she certainly didn't care what other people thought about her. Not as long as she had me.

And then, sometime around ninth grade, she did a complete 180. It was amazing, really. She met Mark, now her husband, and the next thing I knew, she was experimenting with makeup and asking my advice on fashion, even borrowing my clothes, which annoyed me no end. She had become a whole new person and, I had to admit, I had a hard time relating to her. Jealousy was part of it. I felt as if Mark had slid right into my place of importance.

Jill and Mark went steady all through high school and college and then got married and started a family. She never went out with anyone else. And after they got together we were never as close as we'd been before. She didn't need me anymore.

I could still see the messy little tomboy she used to be, but it was almost as if that were another sister. Now there was no remnant of that person. Now she wore black trousers with a gold chain-link belt, white silk blouse and gold hoop earrings. Her chin-length hair was perfectly highlighted and she brushed her shiny thick bangs off her forehead with a manicured forefinger. I was fashionable—after all, it was my business—but much more casual in jeans tucked into knee-high boots and a rather low-cut red top, my frizzy hair pulled back with a ribbon and little corkscrew curls popping out all over the place.

"You look terrific," I told Jill. "Going somewhere this afternoon?"

"Your belated birthday lunch," she said. "And then my bridge club." Or Junior League or the PTA or the volunteer work she did at the library. Jill always had a million things going on.

The waiter came by, a twenty-something with gelled and spiked hair, blue eyes and tattoos starting at both wrists and disappearing under the sleeves of his T-shirt.

"My name is Jarrod and I'll be your server. You ladies are looking lovely today," he said, which could have sounded sleazy but seemed immensely sincere, probably because of his youth and his bright white smile. Obsequiousness and flirtation, an excellent combination for someone hoping to score a big tip from two older ladies.

"How's the Caesar salad?" I asked.

"Fab. We use white anchovies and shaved fresh Parmesan. But if you want the best thing on the menu, this is it," he said, and bent close to point to the portobello mushroom sandwich. He smelled faintly of herbal shampoo. "It's marinated and grilled, and has goat cheese, caramelized onions and fire-roasted red pepper on a ciabatta roll. And I recommend the sweet potato fries, although you can get the hand-cut French fries if you want."

Under his spell I ordered exactly as he suggested. Jill ordered an omelet and we both ordered a glass of wine, the Côtes du Rhône because he said it was crisp and elegant. Was he even old enough to drink it?

"So," Jill said when he'd gone, "why didn't you tell me Michael proposed?"

"I didn't have time. He sprung that ring on me and then he sprung the news on everyone at that stupid surprise party. It was crazy."

"He was pretty excited about that party. He had us all believing you'd be thrilled by it."

"I'm not sure I like this new Michael," I said. "I thought we were on the same page about things like marriage and living together. And even surprise parties. I mean, he blindsided me with that ring." I told her how he'd proposed at the restaurant and then about our fight. "I haven't talked to him in days, and we usually talk at least once a day. He's pouting, I think."

"Why don't you call him?" she said.

Jarrod the waiter brought our wine. "Everything okay here?" he asked.

It would be, I thought, if I wasn't fifty and pseudo-engaged. "Perfect," I said and he rewarded me with a big, toothy smile.

"Your lunch will be ready in a few minutes."

"He likes you," Jill said as he walked away.

"I could be his mother," I said, secretly pleased.

"Do you think you're having a midlife crisis?" Jill asked.

"Oh, fuck you," I said and she laughed.

"Being fifty sucks, doesn't it?" she said.

"More than you know. Just wait. You'll see."

"Seriously, though, I think you should call Michael. Don't let this fester."

"He can call me, too, you know."

"Lib, don't stand on ceremony here. This is the rest of your life you're talking about. Michael's the best guy you've ever been with. Don't let that go."

The waiter brought our food, so I didn't have to answer, but I resented Jill for siding with Michael. She was my sister; wasn't she supposed to be on my side?

I took a bite of my portobello sandwich, which was delicious, but now I wasn't hungry. Jill took one of my sweet potato fries. "You've had some bad luck with men in the past, but Michael's someone you can grow old with," she said.

I could see Michael and me sitting in matching easy chairs in a nursing home somewhere, wiping drool off each other's chins. But I couldn't see what led up to it. I couldn't see us married and living together. "Maybe to you he's the best guy I've ever been with, but you don't live with us and I'm not so sure. Our relationship is fine. It's nice," I said. "It's easy. It's comfortable. But is that reason enough to marry him? Shouldn't it be more . . . thrilling, more passionate?"

"People get married for different reasons," Jill said. "And I think at our age we have different priorities." She took a cheesy bite of her omelet. "I always thought Michael was your Mr. Right. You seem happy with him."

"I am happy with him, the way things are. I'm not so sure we would work as a married couple. Sometimes I feel like I'm a different person when I'm with Michael."

"Maybe you are, but is that bad?" Jill asked. "You're more settled. That's a good thing."

"*Settled.* God, that's so boring."

"Lib, that's what marriage is all about, at least the good ones. It's about being settled and comfortable with someone, having someone to count on."

I took another bite of my sandwich and wiped my mouth, realizing I'd inhaled three-quarters of it without even tasting it.

"I've got Rufus."

"Rufus has his limitations."

"Maybe," I said. "But cats are so much more reliable than men. He loves me no matter what. He never makes me feel bad about myself, he approves of everything I do, he doesn't leave toast crumbs on the table."

Jill said, "He doesn't blow his nose in the shower, he doesn't leave the coffeepot on the edge of the counter after he makes coffee."

"He doesn't fold my collar down when I intentionally, and stylishly, leave it up. He doesn't throw away the newspaper before I've finished it."

We both laughed even though I was half serious. Fact was, I wanted to be finished with this conversation. I didn't want any more advice from my little sister, who lived in storybook land, who'd lucked out at fifteen and met her Prince Charming and lived happily ever after.

But Jill wasn't finished. She put down her fork and leaned toward me, putting her hand on mine. "All that cleverness aside, you've had the passionate, tumultuous relationships, and how did those work for you?"

I bristled, and pulled my hand away. "Shit happens, Jill. Not everyone's as lucky in love as you. Just because other relationships haven't worked out doesn't mean this one's right.

It's been right for a couple of years at this time in my life, but that doesn't make it right for eternity."

Jill kept her mouth shut then. Sometimes, not often, but sometimes she knew when to quit. We ate in silence for a bit as I tried to think of a neutral subject. I thought about telling her about Patrick but ruled that out. I could just hear her: *"Don't throw away your life with Michael for some fantasy,"* she'd say, I was sure.

"Maybe you should try putting out a different vibe into the universe," Jill said. "A vibe of being grateful and happy with what you've got."

"Yeah, Jill, I'll put out a *vibe into the universe.*" Jesus. "You know what? I am grateful for my life; I have a wonderful life that I'm very happy with. That has nothing to do with anything. I don't need to send out a fucking *vibe.* In fact, don't you think that proves my point? I'm happy with my life and I don't need a man to make me feel that way. And getting married isn't going to make me any happier or more grateful than I already am, is it?"

The whole conversation made me feel like I had as a kid when my mother told me that beets and Brussels sprouts had important nutrients and fiber that would make me stronger and give me more energy for the track team. They both grossed me out, so I'd move them around on my plate or spit them into a napkin when she wasn't looking. When I made the team it was all I could do not to say, "See, I did it without those stupid vegetables."

Jill drank the last of her wine and sat back, silent. Okay, let her pout, I thought.

But she's my little sister. "So who's in your bridge club?" I asked, knowing she'd be unable to resist talking about her perfect life and her perfect friends.

I felt wistful for the messy little girl she once was, the one who looked up to me and envied my life, who thought I was great and who wanted to be just like me.

As Jill talked I finished my wine and signaled my boyfriend Jarrod for another glass.

Thirteen

─◦ ❧ ◦─

I don't believe in signs from above. I don't. But I was finishing my run that crisp clear morning, making my way past raked leaves and neatly edged lawns, and when I turned onto Cherry Street I saw a big For Sale sign standing self-importantly in front of my favorite house. I almost ran into a tree. When is a sign a sign? Well, this one was accompanied by an insistent little voice telling me that some things are *meant to be*; Michael and I were meant to get married, meant to buy this house, meant to live happily ever after.

Fuck that little voice.

When I got home the answering machine light was blinking. I hoped it was finally Michael. His silence was beginning to piss me off. It now seemed like a standoff and the one who called first would be the weakling.

But it wasn't Michael, it was Patrick, and as I listened to his message, relief and affection spread through me like warm milk.

"Hey, I had a great idea," his once-again familiar voice said. "I was thinking I'd come to Chicago and take you to lunch. What do you think? No pressure. No stress. We'll just have lunch and then I'll go home. Doesn't that sound like fun? It would be great to see you."

Come to Chicago? For lunch? It was outrageous. But my heart was thumping when the message ended. Was he serious? It was so impulsive, so daring, so extraordinary. So unlike anything that ever happened in my life.

I dialed his number. "Okay, do I need to remind you that you live a thousand miles away?"

"Hey!" he said, clearly happy to hear from me.

"That's a tough commute for lunch."

"It's not so bad," he said. "It's just a quick plane ride." His enthusiasm made me feel young and reckless. "So when should I come? Tomorrow?"

"Oh, god no, not tomorrow for heaven's sake!" I said, feeling an equal measure of elation and terror.

"Just kidding," he said. "But how about Friday? Would that work for you?" I felt a giggle rising up from my stomach as I looked at my calendar. I had someone coming in for a fitting on Friday, then a dentist appointment, then a phone consultation. The fitting was at nine A.M. The others? Was my life all about fittings and appointments and obligations? Why couldn't they be rescheduled? How could I not rearrange a few things for Patrick's amazing idea?

"Friday could work," I found myself saying. Was I really going to let him do this?

"Outstanding," Patrick said. "I'll e-mail the details."

After we hung up I stood there grinning like a goofball, thoughts racing around my brain like Ping-Pong balls. I imagined us eating lunch at the airport amid the hustle and bustle of travelers. Would it be awkward? What would he look like in the flesh? Would we be as comfortable face-to-face as we were on the phone? Should I call my hairdresser and evict the gray? Could I lose five pounds by Friday? Maybe get a quick shot of Botox?

The part of me that wasn't overwhelmed was inflated like a joyous bubble. I was going to see Patrick Harrison.

I had to tell Sophie.

"You're kidding," she said when I called her. "He's coming to Chicago just for lunch? How fun. And decadent. Can Pete and I come?"

"No!" I said.

She laughed. "Kidding," she said. "He e-mailed Pete. Pete was really excited to hear from him. He said we should plan a trip to Florida to visit."

"Let's all go. A road trip, just like that time we all drove to St. Louis, remember? In our senior year?"

"I remember," Sophie said. "I remember that ratty motel we stayed in."

"Remember those Missouri cockroaches? They were big as cats. Patrick went after one with his boot and it got right up and ran away."

"That was so much fun, wasn't it? If you could go back to that time, would you?"

"For the day, maybe, but to live it all again? I don't think so. Would you?"

"Would I be able to do anything different?" she asked. It was a totally unexpected response.

"What would you want to do differently? Oh my god, if you're going to tell me you and Pete are having problems, what chance in hell do I have of a decent relationship?"

"No, no, we're good. But if I could do it again, I'd maybe go to law school before we had kids. And work for a couple years. Sometimes I wish I had a career I could have fallen back on."

"You always seemed content to be a stay-at-home mom."

"I know. I was. I am. Pretty much. But I always envied your having a career, working your way up in the corporate world, earning the boss's respect, that sense of accomplishment. Not to mention wearing beautiful clothes."

I narrowed my eyes. "Somehow I don't see you as a lawyer."

"Yeah, well, maybe a veterinarian, then. Or tennis pro."

"Or storm-chaser," I said. "Or Barbie-dress designer."

We both laughed but then Sophie got serious again. "And then you started your own business," she said, "and made a success of that. I guess if I had it to do again, I'd just have wanted something of my own, outside of the family. I'm sorry I didn't have that experience."

"How did I not know that?" It seemed disheartening to me that we'd been friends for almost forty years and I hadn't known this about her. How do you ever really know someone? "You could still do it, you know. You could go back to school if you wanted to. Or start a business."

"Oh sure, just like that."

"If you're serious, Soph, I'll work on it with you. You have lots of talent you could turn into a business; you're an amazing cook, your arts and craft stuff. . . ."

"It's not that big of a deal. Really. Just a small regret in my otherwise marvelous life. Just something I've thought about recently, especially now that Danielle's getting married. Pretty soon Tiffany will be going off to college, and then what will I do?"

"Go to the spa? Eat bonbons?"

"Oh hell, I've been doing that for years," she said. "So anyway, I hate to rain on your parade but what about this lunch with Patrick? Are you going to tell Michael?"

"Michael?"

"Michael."

"Oh god, Sophie, I don't know. It's just lunch. Why do I have to worry about Michael now?"

"Because you're engaged, even if you're not sure you want to be, and you're going to have lunch with your high school sweetheart who's traveling twelve hundred miles to see you. That's why."

"Oh," I said. "Yeah, there's that."

Fourteen

$\sim\!\!\sim\!\!\forall\!\!\sim$

I'd been circling O'Hare for eighteen minutes, checking arrival times on my iPhone. When I knew Patrick's plane had landed I pulled up to Arrivals and watched people filing through the doors of the terminal, looking for a current-day Patrick. Clusters of people rushed out and I scanned them, but then the crowds slowed and people trickled out in ones and twos. I pulled down my visor and checked myself in the mirror to make sure there was no lipstick on my teeth. What would Patrick think when he saw me? How did I compare with the me he knew so many years ago? Would he even recognize me?

A man about the right age walked out and looked up and down the row of waiting cars. My heart thumped as I studied him, but unless Patrick had put on fifty pounds since his picture was taken (a possibility that hadn't occurred to me), it wasn't him. I blew out a breath when the man walked away. I glanced in the mirror again, checked my makeup and hair. Several more men came out of the terminal, but two of them were too young and the third was a large black man in a

UCLA jacket. I drummed my fingers on the steering wheel and fluffed the hair at the back of my neck.

A tall, distinguished man in a trench coat walked quickly out to the curb as a beautiful woman got out of the Mercedes in front of me. They kissed tenderly. He pulled back, looked deeply into her eyes and broke into a wide grin. I smiled as the woman put her hand on his cheek. She was elegantly dressed in a long charcoal-gray coat over an ivory turtleneck, her hair pulled into a lovely chignon. I wished I looked as elegant. After all the clothes I'd tried on, I'd settled on tan trousers with a cream-colored sweater and short tweed jacket. Was it too dressy? Did it look like I was trying too hard? Maybe the chunky gold necklace was too much. I took it off and threw it in my purse.

I'd worked late into last night, too keyed up to sleep. I'd finished altering two pairs of pants and ripped apart a jacket before feeling tired enough to go to bed. And then I'd fallen asleep at once, only to awaken an hour later. This was worse than high school.

And all night Michael's face rose up in my mind along with the hurt he would feel over what I was doing. What if he found out? What if he just happened to be meeting a friend at the airport at exactly the same time and we ran into each other and he saw me with Patrick?

A man and a woman came out of the terminal and chatted at the door. The woman was plump and wore a long black cape. She had tight silver curls and threw her head back to laugh, the breath floating from her mouth in a plume. The man wore a turtleneck and sport coat but no overcoat. Then they shook hands and the woman walked toward the taxi stand. The man stood for a moment looking around. My breath quickened as he started for my car, smiling. In the few seconds before I opened my door to get out I saw that this new Patrick was quite different from the boy of eighteen with long dark hair and black leather. His hair was still on the long side, not quite reaching his collar, and was more gray than brown. His face was fuller and his body heavier, but thankfully not by fifty pounds. He wore no leather, no chains, just that big smile and shining eyes. I swallowed hard.

He grinned when I walked around the car to the passenger side and we stood looking at each other. You know those age-progression photos, the ones that age a runaway child into a teen? Well, that's what it was like looking at him. He was there, the Patrick of old, but whitewashed with this new face; softer, less angular, more cozy looking. His eyes had faint creases in the corners.

Sophie would be saying, *Look at him, Libby. Just* look *at him. He's gorgeous.*

He studied my face, my hair, my mouth. "Unbelievable," he said, and we laughed.

"Good unbelievable or bad unbelievable?" I asked, even though the answer was painted clearly in his eyes. And that made us laugh even more. We couldn't seem to stop laughing and people turned to look at us, chuckling. Patrick opened his arms and I folded into him, wrapping my arms around his substantial fifty-something body. He held me for a moment, kissed me on the cheek, then pulled back and looked deeply into my eyes. He smiled. Just like the guy with the Mercedes woman. I was completely charmed. I felt like I had in high school the first time he asked me out. I could see his admiration back then, too, and it had puffed me up with pleasure.

We decided to drive downtown and take a walk before finding someplace for lunch. "Aren't you cold?" I asked as we walked on the lakefront path.

"Not bad," he said. "Why? Are you?"

"No, I'm fine. See this thing I'm wearing? It's called a coat. It's a great little invention."

"I got rid of mine when I moved to Florida and swore I'd never buy another," Patrick said. "I turned the house upside down looking for this turtleneck."

"When we were in high school you always wore black turtlenecks, do you remember?" I asked.

"I think we both always wore them."

"I wore them because you did and you looked so cool and I wanted to be cool, too."

He laughed and put his arm around me for a second, and I had to work at keeping a big, dopey grin off my face. He hugged me to him quickly and then let me go. No, I thought, don't let go.

Our conversation was light and casual, and there was no mention of Michael, thank god. I kept sneaking glances at Patrick, getting used to how he looked now. The boy I knew was in there; he moved with the same familiar, relaxed grace and his eyes still wrinkled up at the corners when he smiled.

We talked about his flight, security at the airport, the weather in Chicago, the weather in Florida. We talked about the traffic on the Kennedy Expressway on the way into town. We filled an awkward silence with a discussion about the temperature of Lake Michigan and how calm it was today. Patrick seemed more recognizable as we walked, his gestures, his expressions, his smile.

"Hungry?" I asked.

"Starved," he said.

The Cheesecake Factory was packed with Michigan Avenue shoppers and tourists. There would be a forty-five-minute wait for a table.

"Want to go somewhere else?" I asked.

"No, I'm fine with waiting," Patrick said. "It's part of the Chicago experience. Where I live you can walk into any restaurant, sit right down, order and eat, including dessert and coffee, in about half an hour."

We went to the bar and Patrick ordered us Bloody Marys.

"Do you like small-town living?"

"Yeah, I do," he said. "I like knowing everyone. I like how simple it is. It's a different life, that's for sure." Very different from my own.

When the bartender brought our drinks we clinked glasses and drank to our reunion.

"You look even better in person," Patrick said. "You're definitely aging gracefully. And I like the gray in your hair. It looks great."

I flushed at his compliments. "Thanks," I said. "I considered coloring it this morning before you got here but ran out of time."

"I'm glad," he said. "So, bring me up to date on the last thirty-two years."

I gave him the CliffsNotes version of my college years, my two marriages and my midlife career change. I told him about some of my clients, about Sophie and Pete and their girls. He told me about his ex-wife, how he got started in the kayaking business, how he'd taught his son to fish and play guitar. "I told Ashley and his wife about how we reconnected and that I was coming to see you. They got a kick out of it."

I would have loved to have heard that conversation. It pleased me that he told them, that they knew about me.

Patrick pulled a skewered blue cheese–stuffed olive out of

his drink and offered it to me. My eyes lit up and I plucked it off and popped it in my mouth.

"You don't like blue-cheese olives?" I asked.

"No, I love them. But you went after yours like it was gonna get up and run away, so I figured you like them more than I do."

I laughed, happily chomping.

"So how is it some woman hasn't snatched you up?" I said.

"I don't know," he said. "Amazing, isn't it? I'm such a catch."

"You look good on paper, but you never know, do you? Do you snore?"

"Probably, but it doesn't keep me awake," he said. "Actually, I lived with someone for about five years but ultimately it didn't work out."

"When was that?"

"A couple years ago."

"What happened?"

Patrick laughed. "Don't be shy, Libby. Just get right to the point here."

"Sorry," I said, feeling chastened. "You don't have to answer. I'm just curious. Just tell me to shut up."

"I'm kidding," he said, and his grin loosened my shoulders. "I don't mind. My life's an open book."

"Okay, so why didn't it work?"

He laughed again. "We just had different interests. At first it didn't seem to matter but after a while it got to be a problem. She was ambitious, a corporate hotshot. I don't think I was the right image for her. Not that she ever said that," he said. "She was really sweet but our relationship just sort of fizzled out."

"Do you date much?"

"Haven't recently," he said. I smiled inside.

When the hostess came by to tell us our table was ready, Patrick said, "Saved by the bell," and put his hand gently on my back as we followed her to our table. She smiled prettily at him as she handed him a menu. Her shiny blond hair hung in a satiny spill to her waist and she wore a cropped top and tight black hip-hugger bell-bottoms.

"Didn't you used to have an outfit like that?" Patrick asked.

As we shared a piece of turtle cheesecake for dessert I thought how easy it was to be with him. It didn't feel awkward; there were no uncomfortable silences. It was almost as if no time had passed at all.

"I always thought you were pretty, Libby, but you're even prettier now. Your face has more character."

" 'Character' is just a euphemism for 'wrinkles,' " I said.

"Wrinkles mean life. They tell a story. I think faces are so much more interesting when we get older."

"I think faces are so much older when we get older."

His face and arms were browned from the sun. He had a familiar small chip in his right front tooth that was so endearing. I wasn't sure if he was really handsome or if I was simply reacting to our history, but I liked looking at him.

He leaned forward and took my hand. "I'm really glad you e-mailed me," he said.

"Me too," I said. "I was so happy you remembered me."

"Oh Libby, how could I not remember you? Unless I'd been in a coma. I have to say, it's great seeing you after all these years." He picked up his glass. "To reunions," he said, and we sipped our drinks. The whole thing seemed like a dream.

Then Patrick asked, "How are things with Michael?" The question crashed like a steamroller through the fog of my trance.

"Ooh, a dose of reality," I said. I took a tiny bite of cheese-cake. "Frankly, I feel a little guilty being here with you. That's how things are with Michael."

"I'm sorry," he said. "Not sorry because you're here with me, sorry you're feeling guilty. I want you to enjoy this re-union."

"I am. Very much. That's why I'm feeling guilty, I guess."

"I suppose that's a good sign, then. For me, anyway." He grinned, that sweet recognizable grin. I was glad he didn't ask any more about Michael. I didn't really want to think about him right now.

After lunch we walked down Michigan Avenue and looked in the store windows. Patrick pointed out things he thought I'd look good in, and mostly they were things I'd pick out for myself. Except for the slinky, low-cut black sequined dress with spaghetti straps and a thigh-revealing slit.

"Thirty years ago, maybe," I said. "Not today."

"You could pull it off," he said. I couldn't. But I loved that he thought I could.

We bought caramel corn at Garrett's and munched on it as we made our way down to the Chicago River and on over to State Street. We went into Macy's and Patrick lamented the fact that it was no longer Marshall Field's. "My mom used to bring all us kids down here when we were little to see the Christmas windows and eat in the Walnut Room."

"They still do the windows."

"Not the same," he said and I agreed.

We wandered through the men's department, where Patrick picked up a package of jockey shorts and some socks.

"What, they don't have underwear in Florida?"

He smiled. "Let's go find me another turtleneck," he said. I stopped. "Patrick. What are you doing?"

He faced me with a mischievous smile and a twinkle in

his eye. "I was thinking I'd stay the night just on the off-chance I could see you again tomorrow."

My heart thumped against my rib cage. My mouth went dry. I was thrilled. And panicked. "You said lunch. You said we'd have lunch and then you'd leave. You promised."

He put his hand on my shoulder. "I'm scaring you, aren't I?" I nodded. "I'm sorry. I don't want to cause trouble. Look, I'll put these back." He turned around and put the black socks on a rack of white ones. I resisted the urge to put them in the right place. "If you want me to go, I'll go. I promised and I meant it. I will. But I don't want to. I don't want to leave you yet."

"It's not that I want you to go," I said. "It's just that . . ."

"Look, I'll stay one night. I don't have to get back for anything, so it's no big deal for me. So I'll just stay. We'll talk tomorrow. And then if you want me to go home, I'll go. I promise."

"I've heard *that* before," I said.

He smiled. "Yeah, I know. Another promise. But I mean it. No pressure. I swear, if you don't want to see me tomor-row, I'll go home. You don't even have to call me. If I don't hear from you by noon, I'll leave. And no hurt feelings." He put his hand on my shoulder again. "What do you say? It's your call."

Why not? All I had to do was not call him tomorrow and he'd be gone. I had the whole rest of the evening and all night to think about it. Not that there was much doubt in my mind.

I picked up the package of socks and handed it to him. "Let's go find you a turtleneck," I said, and he broke into a heartbreakingly adorable, chip-toothed grin.

It was fun walking through the store together, holding hands, looking for all the world as if we were a couple. I was aware of people looking at us and imagined their envy. They were thinking we looked good together. They were thinking how nice it was that we were still in love after all these years now that our children were grown and gone. They were thinking, Look at these old people holding hands. Isn't that sweet?

Patrick put his arm around me as we walked away from the register, and the sales girl smiled at us.

"Have a nice evening," she said brightly as if she knew something.

⟁

I pulled up in front of the Palmer House hotel and a doorman hurried over to Patrick's door. Patrick put up one finger and turned back to me. "Well, girl," he said, "this has been one ass-kickin' kind of day."

I laughed. "That's not exactly how I would have described it, but it has definitely been some kind of day."

"Some kind of good?"

"Some kind of good."

He took my hand in his and kissed it. *Kissed it.*

"Libby," he began, but then he stopped and shook his head. "Libby, Libby, Libby." He leaned over and kissed my mouth. I remembered those lips. His kiss was like a familiar song, and as it played my brain was flooded with memories. A song, that's what his kiss was like.

He pulled back and looked at me, and a smile lit up his eyes and infused his whole face. "This is wild," he said. "It's my fantasy."

His fantasy. I almost giggled, like a nervous teenager.

He swept his hand across my cheek, and then kissed me again, more insistently now, with mouth open, moist and cushiony. And I kissed him back, and put my hand on his cashmered chest.

And the doorman stood there waiting to open the door.

I remembered this about Patrick: he was a great kisser.

"I'm just not ready to let you go," he said. I wasn't ready either. It was the last thing I wanted to do. "Why don't you let the valet take your car and come have a drink with me?"

I put that car right in park. "Lead the way," I said.

As Patrick checked in at reception, I told him I'd wait in the bar while he put his things in the room. "Chicken," he said as I turned and walked away.

He was right. I was chicken. But there was no way I was going to be alone in a room with just him and me and a bed.

Fifteen

─◌ ⚘ ◌─

"C ome here often?" Patrick said, startling me as I sat at the bar sipping a glass of wine. The room was dimly lit and if you didn't know it was four in the afternoon you'd think it was midnight. There were only two other people at the bar, and one person sat at a table talking on a cell phone and taking notes.

"How's your room?" I asked after Patrick ordered a beer.

"Nice," he said. "Want to see?"

Yes. "No way."

"Okay, okay," he said. "I'll stop." But I didn't really want him to; I liked the sexual banter. It made me feel sexy and desirable. It made me feel like a teenager.

"Okay, here's the deal," I told him. "I have dinner plans tonight, so I have to be out of here no later than six." I didn't have dinner plans. I had no plans at all. But it seemed like a good idea for him to think so. It felt like I could get into trouble so easily. Here I was fifty years old and I was making up a story because I didn't trust myself to be alone with him.

"Great," he said. "We've got almost two hours."

We sipped our drinks and reminisced about high school.

We talked about Sophie and Pete and how great it was that they were still together.

"Remember senior prom? The four of us going to North Avenue Beach at four in the morning? I still remember the dress you wore."

"You do not," I said.

"It was blue and long and had rhinestone straps. And your shoes matched perfectly. I think they even had something rhinestone on them, didn't they?"

I narrowed my eyes at him. "Are you gay?"

He laughed. "Just a good memory."

"You're amazing. My mom had those shoes dyed to match. And she put rhinestone clip-on earrings on them. I can't believe you remember that."

"I remember everything. I remember how we used to meet at the parking lot before school."

"Me too. I was grounded after New Year's, so you couldn't pick me up. Do you remember?" He nodded. "So I'd take the bus and meet you in the parking lot."

"Where we'd make out like mad until the bell rang and then we'd run like hell to make it to homeroom."

"My parents never did get to know you."

"They hated my long hair and black leather."

"I wonder what they'd think today."

"They'd probably think my hair was still too long. And that I needed a real job."

As Patrick ordered us another drink I watched him in the mirror over the bar, chatting with the bartender, finding out his name, asking him to recommend a seasonal beer. He had a friendly, relaxed manner about him.

I was feeling heady from the wine, but mostly just drunk with the whole idea of Patrick Harrison here, now, and I giggled.

"What?" he said, taking my hand.

"This is just so strange."

"I know," he said and kissed me, once, and then again. "Like a couple of kids."

"We used to make out in the parking lot at school and here we are, fifty years old, making out at a bar in downtown Chicago," I said.

"We're not exactly making out," he said. "But I'd be happy to oblige." He said this with an exaggerated leer. I felt happy inside, like someone who'd just won a blue ribbon.

"People are looking at us," I said.

"Do you care?"

"Not really," I said. And I didn't. Unless someone who knew Michael was here.

For a while we sat silently, sipping our drinks. Patrick seemed easy and comfortable. I wished I could jump into his brain and find out what he was thinking. He ran his pinky along the back of my hand. We looked at each other in the mirror over the bar.

"Why'd we break up?" Patrick asked.

"I don't think we did. At least I don't remember any big scene. Do you? You're the one who remembers everything."

"I don't."

"I went away to college. I think that's what happened. We called each other for a while but it was tough being so far away."

"We were stupid. We shouldn't have let it go."

In my head I said, *"So, wanna go up to your room?"* and off we'd go to ravage each other like sex-crazed maniacs and profess our undying love.

Instead I looked at my watch. "Oh shit. It's six-thirty," I said.

"How'd that happen?"

I put on my coat and kissed him. "I've got to go." I was virtuous with my resolve, all the while imagining us doing wicked things to each other.

He put his arm around me and walked me to the door while I inwardly argued with myself about leaving. What would happen if I stayed? Would that be so terrible? What was so great about being virtuous anyway?

"So, I'm not going to call you, remember?" he said. "If you want to see me, call me in the morning. Otherwise I'll just head home."

"I remember," I said.

He kissed the top of my head. "So do you think you'll do that?"

Of course.

"You'll just have to wait and see."

Sixteen

~⌒∾ ❦ ∾⌒~

There are few things as jarring as a phone ringing in the middle of the night. Who would call me at 3:51 A.M.? I jolted awake, my heart racing. But then I smiled, sure it was Patrick. Of course it was Patrick.

"Couldn't sleep for thinking about me?" I asked.

"Libby," my mom said. "Can you come over?"

I sat up, my chest thumping. "What is it? Are you okay?" I was already out of bed, stripping off my pajamas, pulling on underwear.

"It's Daddy. Something's wrong." Her voice was filled with confusion, anguish.

My head pounded. I dug my knuckle into my temple. "Did you call 911?" I asked as I pulled on jeans, zipping them, looking around for my shoes.

"I didn't know what to do."

Oh god. "I'll call them, Mom. Hang up, okay? I'll call them and then I'll be right there." A small sound escaped her throat. I made my voice calm to hide my fear. "He'll be okay, Mom," I said, but I didn't feel that optimism in my bones. I walked back and forth in front of the dresser, pounding my thigh with my fist. "Hang up, now. I'll be right there."

My hand shook as I punched in 911 and choked out the address. I knew I had to keep it together for my mother, but as I tied my shoes a wail gathered in my throat. Please, no. Not yet. Let him be all right.

I wasn't ready. I still needed my father. It didn't matter that I was fifty years old. At that moment I felt ten. Six. Five years old.

Daddy.

❦

Lights from the ambulance strobed the neighborhood as I drove up. Two men were lifting a stretcher down the porch steps. My mother held my father's hand, running alongside in quick little steps as they moved toward the waiting vehicle. He looked fine when I got to him, just sleeping. I touched his cheek. "I love you, Daddy," I whispered, wishing for a finger twitch or the tremble of an eyelid. If he were dead they'd be carrying him out completely covered by the sheet, I thought, and took solace in that.

"I'll be right behind you," I told my mother as the EMT helped her into the ambulance. "I'll get you some clothes." She was oblivious that she was in her blue chenille bathrobe— she probably wouldn't care even if she did realize it—but it was something useful I could do.

At the hospital, little clusters of people stood and sat in the waiting room: a woman with wiry gray hair and three children wearing Chicago Cubs caps; a young couple with black hair, black lipstick, black nail polish and silver posts through their noses. And my mother, sitting alone, looking very small, turned in on herself, hands folded in her lap, head down. I stood in the doorway afraid to talk, afraid to move. I had a bad feeling. How could I comfort her? Who was going to comfort me?

She looked up then, her whole being overflowing with sadness. I sat beside her, hugged her, patted her hair down, put my hand on hers.

"I called Jill," I said. "She and Mark are on the way."

She nodded.

"I brought you some clothes." I pointed to the paper bag on the floor but I could see it wasn't registering. "Doesn't matter," I said and we sat in silence, Mother's foot tapping softly in her slipper.

"What happened?" I asked.

She slumped forward and put her face in her hands. I rubbed her bony back. "I don't know. He moaned in his sleep. I thought he was dreaming and I went back to sleep." Her voice cracked.

"Shhhh," I said. "You couldn't know, Mom." She sat back and I put my arm around her. She was trembling.

"But then something woke me. He was so still." Tears fell down her cheeks. "I should have done something earlier. If he doesn't make it it's my fault."

"No, Mom. It'll be all right. He'll pull through." What else could I say? I rubbed her shoulder, wishing someone were there to rub mine.

And then, thankfully, Jill and Mark rushed in looking like they'd just gotten out of bed, which, of course, they had. I almost cried with relief at seeing them. And right behind them was Michael. The sight of his face took my breath away. I was surprised by his presence but glad Jill had called him. He scooped me up in a big, protective hug and I melted into his chest. He smelled like Michael, a clean, sleepy smell.

"You okay?" he asked and I nodded. He cupped my head with his hand and I exhaled. "He'll come out of this, Lib. He's going to be fine."

His sureness settled around me like a safety net.

Seventeen

—◦ ❦ ◦—

It's not that I didn't think about Patrick. I was certainly aware, somewhere in the recesses of my mind, that he'd left town with the impression I didn't want to see him. But I couldn't let myself consider him when my father had just had a stroke. As I sat by my father's side I could only think that he might never again hear me tell him I loved him. I might never again feel his arms around me or hear his voice or see his smile. I stayed, holding his hand, talking to him when my mother was sleeping or had gone home to bathe and change clothes. Jill was there, too, in and out. She encouraged me to go home, get some rest. "There's nothing you can do here," she told me, but I thought my voice could wake him. I thought if anyone could bring him back, I could. So I kept talking.

"Remember the time you took Jill and me to the Cubs game, Daddy? Remember the bobble-head dolls you bought us? I still have mine." I did. It sat on a shelf in my workroom next to my favorite family photo, taken when Jill and I were just toddlers in little ruffled sunsuits.

"How about that time I hit a grand slam when I was ten

and we won the game and the league championship? Remember that? I know you do. You honked the horn all the way to Baskin-Robbins and bought the biggest sundae they made, with all my favorite flavors, and the four of us toasted me on every spoonful. Do you remember? It had butter pecan, chocolate chocolate chip, rocky road . . . what else? Did it have turtle ice cream, too? It had chocolate sauce, caramel sauce, raspberry. It had everything! And then it had mounds of whipped cream and a cherry on top. Do you remember that, Daddy? It was gross. And we ate the whole thing. I couldn't look at ice cream for a year after that."

I watched closely for the slightest tremor, an acknowledgment that he heard. But there was nothing, no movement. He looked small and vacant lying there.

I thought about what he'd said after Michael announced our engagement—about not having to worry about me anymore—so I told him how great Michael had been during this time, how he'd brought me clean clothes, homemade sandwiches, soup in a thermos.

"He never tells me I should go home. He knows I need to be here. He comes and goes. Sometimes he sits with me and makes sure I eat something and then he kisses me and leaves and comes back again later. He's been my rock, my anchor. You're right, Dad, you won't have to worry about me after Michael and I are married. He's a good man."

I thought if only he would just wake up now, I'd marry Michael tomorrow and he would walk me down the aisle.

Sophie and Tiffany came by. Sophie brought magazines and books, *The Kite Runner* and *To Kill a Mockingbird*, but I couldn't concentrate enough to read. She went to my house and made macaroni and cheese and lasagna, and made sure Rufus's litter box was scooped and that he had food and water. She checked my e-mail and responded to clients for me.

"There was an e-mail from Patrick," she said.

"What did it say?" For a second I was back at the bar at the Palmer House, holding hands with him, giggling together, feeling something sweet and old—new in the pit of my stomach.

"I didn't read it," she said.

I laughed. "You did, too."

"No, truly, I didn't. It just didn't feel right. But I had Pete e-mail him later to tell him about your dad. I hope that's okay."

"It's fine," I said. I wanted to read that e-mail. But I thought if I denied myself this pleasure my father might wake up.

And on the third day my father did open his eyes. My mother was sitting in the chair by the window, leafing through an old issue of *Better Homes and Gardens.* I was sitting by his bed trying to read *The Kite Runner.* Out of the corner of my eye I saw his finger move and my head snapped up. He was looking at me, his blue eyes soft and confused. I thought he didn't recognize me for a minute and a sharp pain grabbed my chest but then he said, "Hi, pumpkin," and my eyes filled. Oh my god. He was alive. He knew me. He was going to come out of this.

My mother rushed over and took his hand. I touched his arm, his face. Our tears fell on his blanket.

"What happened?" he whispered. "Where . . ."

I pushed the button for the nurse while my mother told him what had happened. As she talked he closed his eyes and a knife of panic stabbed my heart, but when she stopped talking he opened them again. "Don't cry," he said to me, and then, "Tired . . ."

A nurse came in and when she saw my father awake ran back out and called orders to the aides. Suddenly the room was alive with activity and we were asked to please wait in the lounge. I argued, not wanting to leave him, but the nurse gently led me to the door and asked that they be allowed to do their work.

I called Jill and Michael while we waited. When I told Jill he was awake she let out a squeaky "Ooooohhhhh," and I could hear her choking back tears. Michael said, "I'm so glad, Lib. I knew he'd be okay, I just felt it." I was soothed by his words. He said he was rushing over. I called Sophie. I wanted them all: my sister, her husband, her kids, Michael, Sophie, Mark. I wanted everyone there with my mom and me when we saw my father again. I wanted him to know how much he was loved so he would fight to stay with us.

We waited, talking quietly, all of us speculating whether Dad would need to go to rehab, what his condition would be, if he'd have any paralysis, if his brain had been affected.

"We'll hope for the best but prepare for the worst," my mother said in her no-nonsense way. "We'll manage whatever we need to manage."

"One of my clients is a physician who doesn't practice anymore. Now he's a medical consultant," Michael said. "He specializes in elder care and I know he'll be happy to help out. He knows everybody in the industry." Michael smiled tenderly at my mother and she patted his hand with trembling fingers. I put my head on his shoulder and felt a rush of gratitude. Yes, I was grateful. Very, very grateful.

Eighteen

❧ ⚜ ❧

The year I went to college my dad drove me the two hundred miles, my clothes and books and stuffed animals (and my bed pillow) in bins in the backseat. Jill had a piano recital that weekend, so she and my mom stayed behind. I was anxious and a little teary, and aghast at having to travel solo with my dad. In my teenage years I lived in a fog of intolerance for this man I'd previously idolized. At some point (around fourteen or fifteen) I realized I'd grown smarter than him and wasn't shy about updating him as to this new development. I was insufferable then, and didn't see that clearly until I came out on the other side, somewhere in my twenties. Now I could only admire him for getting through that period without throttling me.

Anyway, we didn't have much to talk about on that trip— not his fault, he made the effort, asking me about the dorm and my classes and my new roommate, but it probably felt like riding a bike without the chain, so he let it go after a while and we rode without real conversation. If iPods had been invented back then, I surely would have been hooked up, but I managed to be tuned out just the same, immersed in the radio. We didn't agree on music, of course, and he tolerated Jethro Tull and the Moody Blues far longer than was polite, but when Steven Tyler screamed out his lyrics my dad reached his limit.

"Sorry, Libby, I need some quiet. This is giving me a head-ache."

I shot him a disdainful look and pouted out my window as he shut off the radio.

"Have you decided on your major?" he finally asked, tired, I suppose, of the icy silence.

"No."

"Well, it's early. You've got plenty of time to figure that out. I don't know how you're supposed to decide that when you're eighteen. How can you possibly know now what you want to do the rest of your life?"

"I don't," I said.

"I know."

What he said and his acceptance of my lack of direction surprised me. I saw no hope of figuring it out. It was the burning question, the one that labeled me as the major disappointment of the family. The major disappointment *without* a major. Here I was, off to college, and I didn't even know what I wanted to be. Jill had known for years that she was going to nursing school and was already candy striping at the hospital on weekends.

"When did you know you wanted to be a lawyer?" I asked.

I could almost see his ears perk up, like a terrier, so unaccustomed was he to my asking him a personal question.

"When my mother told me to," he said.

"You did it because your mother told you to?" I was incredulous.

"Well, not exactly. But it was her dream that one of her children would be a lawyer. I'm not sure why, but she talked about it all the while we were growing up, so I guess I just always figured that's what I would do since I was the oldest."

Ah, that's where this is going, I thought. He's going to decide my future.

"So you think I should be a lawyer, is that what you're saying?"

Part of me wanted him to say yes, just to give me another bullet to load into his rifle of uselessness.

He crooked his head at me. "Oh god, no," he said, and after a moment, "unless that's what you want. Do you? Is that what you're considering?"

I pictured myself striding back and forth in front of a jury in a conservative (but fashionably tight) navy blue suit and three-inch heels, waving a pair of horn-rimmed glasses.

"No way," I said, with no small measure of revulsion. "I just thought that's what you were trying to tell me."

"Libby," my dad said, "I want you to do what will make you happy. I want you to find something that gets you out of bed in the morning, something you can't wait to get back to each day. I want you to find your passion."

I had a few friends who had real passions—Kim played the viola and practiced three hours every day, Janet had been studying ballet since she was four, Patrick lived and breathed cars and was working at a body shop—but most of my friends sort of fell into their careers. Pete was majoring in business and knew he'd go to work at his dad's construction company after college, and since Sophie's major was English she thought she'd end up teaching, but neither was what you'd call a passion; they were more like defaults. Most of us were just splashing around in the sea of our future.

"How do I do that?" I asked.

My dad said, "College is going to expose you to a lot of things you never even thought of. Take every course that

sounds interesting and you'll find your passion, you'll see."
This sounded hopeful, and kind of fun, but I doubted the
truth of it. "I know that being a real-estate attorney must
seem very sexy and glamorous"— he looked at me to see if I'd
gotten his little joke —"but I didn't start out with that goal. I
thought I was going to be a litigator. But then I found out I
had no talent for the courtroom." The idea that my father
wasn't competent in everything he ever did had never occurred to me, and it pleased me. "But a law degree opens up a
whole world of possibilities. Not that I'm recommending law
school for you, just college in general. You have no idea the
doors it will open. You're so smart and so talented—"

I snorted. "Yeah, right," I said.

"Don't do that, Libby. It's true. You might not have any
idea right now what you want to do, but you've got plenty of
time to figure it out. And you will. This is just the beginning
and there are all kinds of possibilities out there. You can do
anything you set your mind to."

I was hoping to get through college having fun, making
new friends, drinking a little beer and experimenting with
the requisite amount of illegal substances, and if along the
way I figured out how to fill the vista of blankness that was
my career, well, that would be a bonus. I made a little package of the knowledge that my father hadn't succeeded at the
first thing he'd tried, and put it in a corner of my brain for
safekeeping. It gave me a breather as we drove through small
towns with hardware stores and mom-and-pop groceries on
the way to my vast unknown.

I switched majors twice that first year. I started in jour-
nalism, and my dad bought me a tape recorder and a 35mm
camera to support my choice. When I changed to theater arts
toward the end of my freshman year, I expected him to yank
me out of school faster than the space shuttle launch, but

instead he sent me *An Actor Prepares* and *Building a Character* by Konstantin Stanislavski. He was supportive when I switched to my final major, graphic arts, and when I left the corporate world to start my dressmaking business six years ago he replaced my twenty-five-year-old Singer with a computerized machine with thirty built-in stitches, an LED display and five styles of automatic buttonholes.

Now, as I sat in the waiting room surrounded by the people who meant the most to me, I wondered if he knew the vastness of my appreciation for the father he was. I longed to be able to tell him again how much I appreciated his encouragement, and how remorseful I was for being so truculent on that first ride to college and throughout my teen years. I wanted him to know how his love was the fertilizer that made my life blossom.

Nineteen

━☙ ❦ ❧━

I never saw my father alive again. It wasn't long, maybe an hour or so after we'd all gathered, when the doctor entered the waiting room. All of our heads snapped to the doorway. The doctor hadn't seen us yet and he paused for a moment, removed his glasses and rubbed the bridge of his nose, and then he scanned the room. When he located us he started forward. The skin under his eyes was thin as tissue, and pleated with wrinkles. He had a kind face but there was something in his gaze that pasted me to my seat. I gripped Michael's knee and held my breath while my mother and Jill sprung up as one, standing hopefully in front of him.

"I'm so sorry, Mrs. Carson," the doctor said.

My mother stared. She put her hand to her face. Her mouth opened but no sound emerged.

My stomach was a stone inside me. I looked at Michael in disbelief. I'd just seen my father and he'd looked like he would be all right. How could this be? Tears pooled behind my eyes. *No. No. No.* My breath caught in my throat. I needed to tell him how much I loved him.

I buried my face in Michael's shoulder. *No. No. No. No. No.*

I knew I was lucky to be fifty years old and never to have lost anyone this close to me before. I'd lost an aunt and two uncles and their deaths had left me saddened, but this was an annihilating loss that subsumed me. If my father had had a devastating illness or a long-term slide into senility, I would have at least had time to prepare, but seeing him so healthy and vibrant one day and dead the next left me stunned and reeling, with a liquid anguish running through my veins.

I stayed at my mother's house the days before the funeral, just going home to do the things that needed to be done: calling friends and family to let them know, making funeral arrangements, running errands, trying to keep up with my work. Michael called several of my clients to tell them I'd be unavailable for a while, but I somehow managed to finish all the alterations to Mrs. Rosatti's cruise clothes. I wanted to submerge my mind in the work, but the realization that my father was gone was like a flotation device that kept pulling me up to the surface. More than once I found myself pressing a garment I'd just finished yet couldn't remember doing the work. I did the best I could and simply prayed that everything would fit and be up to my usual quality. Michael delivered everything to Mrs. Rosatti just in time. She was profoundly touched and sent her heartfelt gratitude and condolences.

While at my house I finally read the e-mail from Patrick.

Lib,

I'm so sorry to hear about your dad. I am praying for him to get well and I'm praying for you to be strong. If there's anything I can do, please call me. I know that

**sounds ridiculous—what could I do after all?—but I
do mean it, Lib. My thoughts are with you.**
 Love,
 Patrick

I couldn't tell him my father was dead. I couldn't even
thank him for his kind words. I know it sounds silly—I
know that now—but then it felt like a betrayal to even be
reading the e-mail. It felt like a betrayal of my father, who
believed in my relationship with Michael; it felt like a betrayal of Michael's trust—his love and support. And it felt
like a betrayal of who I was, or thought I should be.

Michael drove me to my mom's each evening and the
three of us sat in the kitchen where Dad's Boston fern hung
over the sink, neglected, trickling leaves. Mom's collection of
Tuscan pottery paraded across the tops of the cabinets and
countertops. I'd always found it odd and sweet that even
though Dad hadn't been a big fan of clutter, he'd had an af-
finity for that collection of pottery. Some years ago he'd
painstakingly painted the chair rail and moldings until they
perfectly matched the forest green in the leaves on the ce-
ramic. It had taken three separate coats before he'd been
satisfied with the color.

On those evenings at Mom's, she made steaming mugs of
hot chocolate and we took them into the den and lit a fire,
and she told us stories of when she and Dad were first married. Michael and I sat side by side on the couch sipping from
sturdy green mugs, Dad's La-Z-Boy mournfully vacant, the
seat cushion lightly dished. I hungered to see him sitting
there, just once more, looking up to smile when I walked in
the room. Just once more was all I wanted.

Then Michael would leave us for the night and Mom and

I would go up to bed. I slept in my old bedroom, which still had lavender walls, the bookshelves Dad had installed and the primitive purple flowers he'd hand-painted on the ceiling.

Night seemed hardest of all with its silence, and the sorrow that pulled at my body. I couldn't imagine how it felt to my mother, lying solitary now in the bed they'd shared for decades, and I wept as much for her as for myself. In the morning I woke to this painful thing inside me, but there was a comfort in seeing my mom and facing the hollowness together.

It didn't feel like my real life while I stayed with her. It felt as if when I finally did return to my own bed in my own house in my normal day-to-day existence, my father might still be there, and I could just call him to grab a cup of coffee with me.

One evening my mother and I sat up long after Michael had gone, poring through photo albums—a vacation in the Wisconsin Dells where Dad smiled out from under a ten-gallon hat as he sat next to a statue of the town sheriff; another at Yellowstone when Jill and I earned patches for being Junior Rangers. There were pictures of family outings and birthdays, anniversaries and graduations. Mom and I shed tears as we turned the pages of memories of picnics and dinners and holidays, but we smiled, too, at the sweet mundane days of my childhood, and laughed over images of Dad as a skinny Santa and Dad in his first pair of Bermuda shorts, proudly displaying his hairy legs for the camera. In most pictures my father had his arm around one of us, and a proud, luminous smile on his face.

"You girls were the pride of his life," Mom said. She had dark circles under her eyes and her hair was uncharacteristically messy, curls spiraling around her head. Exhaustion had etched her face. "Whenever he took you somewhere people would say, 'Here comes Harry and his girls.' He was so proud of that."

"He was a great dad," I said, my voice splintering. Mom touched my cheek. "He was always there when I needed him. He always had good advice."

"Not that you listened," she said.

"That's not true. I listened. I didn't always follow it but I listened. And he was okay with that. He let me do my thing, encouraged me to think for myself."

"He went a bit overboard in that regard," she said with a wisp of a smile. She was the conservative one, wanting me to be safe and knowable. It had been a source of conflict between us when I was young, but they had balanced each other on the parenting scale.

"He never made me feel that anything I wanted to do was silly or beyond me."

"He was less than thrilled when you applied for the Peace Corps," she noted. "Or took up scuba diving."

"But he bought me a customized wet suit."

She leafed through one of the older albums with heavy black pages and white stick-on corners anchoring each photo. She smiled at a black-and-white picture from their first anniversary, Dad looking like a gangster in a pin-striped suit with a wide tie, holding a cigar, and Mom in a dress with forties-style shoulders and a pleated skirt with an orchid pinned to her lapel.

"Look how handsome," she said, a finger caressing Dad's Kodak chest.

"Both of you. You were a beautiful couple."

She sat back, deflated, and her eyes shone with tears. "I don't know how I'm going to live without him," she said, pulling a tissue from her sleeve and wiping her eyes.

"I know," I said. I didn't know how I would either.

In another photo she sat at a table, a big birthday cake in front of her. She leaned forward, blowing out the candles while Dad grinned at the camera.

"My twenty-fifth birthday," she said.

So many years ago, a canyon of memories filled since then. I sighed. "I wish I'd had what you guys had," I said. "All those years together, all that history. I'll never have that."

"Well, you won't be married fifty years but you've started a history with Michael, and you've got lots of time to make memories."

"Sometimes I wish things had worked out with Jeremy and that we'd had a family. We'd have been married thirty years now. I could be a grandmother."

My mother poured more chocolate into my mug and added a cloud of whipped cream. "It doesn't pay to look back, honey," she said.

"I know. But it's hard not to think about it. Daddy was so disappointed when Jeremy and I got divorced. I think he thought I gave up too easily on that marriage."

Mom pulled her sweater tighter around her knobby shoulders. "Perhaps," she said, "but you have to remember we come from a different time, when people stayed together no matter what. But you know he wanted you to be happy. And he always trusted you to do the right thing."

"I know. But still. I envy what you and Dad had. It must give you some comfort now."

"It does. I had fifty-two years with a man I was crazy about." She daintily licked whipped cream off the spoon. "But it wasn't all peaches and cream."

"Well, no relationship is. But you were so in tune, so . . . united."

"We were. But don't idealize it, honey. And don't use it as

a scale to measure your own success or failure. It was human. Real life."

"Of course it was. But it was still an enviable relationship. I want that. Jill managed it, why couldn't I?" I was sounding like a pouty little girl but I couldn't seem to stop myself.

"You and Jill are very different. You wanted different things. She's more like me; traditional, unassuming, wanting peace. You're like Daddy, more of an adventurer. You like to mess things up a bit."

"That's true, but he still had the love of his life," I said, unable to let it go, "and the great relationship. I just sometimes wonder why I couldn't manage that. It seems so basic."

"Libby, stop now. Michael can be your great relationship. Just don't expect it to be like ours or Jill's or anybody else's."

I thought about her words later as I lay in bed unable to sleep, feeling like a forlorn little girl in my childhood bed, wishing to go back to my childhood for just one day. I suppose I did compare my life to theirs. I did always think I'd grow up and get married and have a family and duplicate the template they'd created.

ᴡ

The funeral was on Thursday. I put on a black and gray checked coatdress with black buttons, and brushed out my hair. It hung in soft shiny curls, a good hair day. But it looked like happy hair, so I pulled it back and tied it with a black velvet ribbon.

Michael and I picked up my mother. She walked to the car with her back straight, her hair perfectly done and her blue suit pressed. She hugged me and we held on a little longer than usual. And then she got in the backseat and pulled her skirt down over her knees.

Only the gleaming black hearse was in the parking lot

when we arrived. The funeral home was quiet. Two enormous floral arrangements stood on each side of the glossy casket, and rows of chairs lined up like soldiers. The funeral director was a beefy guy whose muscular arms strained the sleeves of his tasteful navy blue suit coat. He looked like someone who would beat the crap out of you at the slightest provocation, yet he spoke to us in gentle, efficient tones with eyes full of compassion.

Jill and Mark came in, then Sophie, Pete, Danielle and Tiffany, then other friends and family in a steady stream, offering hugs, hands, comforting gestures. Men my father had known since he was in law school hugged me and told me what a good man he was. People I didn't know at all told me how much they would miss him. I felt as if I were playing a role in someone else's life.

"Thank you," I kept saying. "Thank you for coming." Michael stayed by my side, watching me carefully as if afraid I would break. His solicitousness would have normally put me on edge but I felt so insubstantial that his attention seemed to be all that was holding me together.

As I stood to read the eulogy I'd prepared, I looked out at the assembly of friends and family. I wasn't sure I could get through it but was determined to say good-bye to my father. Michael stood behind me, his hand resting on my waist. He'd promised to take over if I couldn't finish.

"When I was three my father took me to his barber for a haircut, unbeknownst to my mother," I read. My mom smiled. "That was my first Buster Brown haircut and it was my signature hairdo until I was ten. Dad always claimed he invented the cut.

"When I was seven I had a concussion and broke my arm in three places when I hit some rocks on my roller skates, and Dad scooped me up and ran with me, on foot, to the emergency room and then stayed by my side until I went home two days later."

I wiped my cheeks with a tissue. Michael whispered, "Do you want me to read?" but I shook my head.

"When I ran my first marathon my dad stationed himself at four different spots along the route to cheer me on with a sign that said, GO LIBBY—THAT'S MY GIRL! and his was the first face I saw when I crossed the finish line."

I broke down then, seeing him in my mind, the pride that had painted his face, his excitement for me, and I gave up the page to Michael. He read on: "He was my biggest fan, and it's unimaginable to me that I'll never again be able to have a conversation with him or hug him or kiss his cheek. He was a good, kind and caring father, and an honorable man, and his greatest pleasure was his family.

"What he has given me is beyond measure, just by being who he was. He taught me about honor and tolerance and acceptance and love. And about commitment and responsibility and goodness and generosity, lessons I am still learning. He will touch me for the rest of my days and I will strive to be more like him. I have cherished every single moment that he was with me. I am so grateful that I've had him for the fifty years of my life."

Michael kissed me and took my hand and we went back to our seats.

I stared out at the expanse of ashen sky as we rode to the cemetery. We were quiet, the air seeming to have been sucked out of us. The earthy smell of the new leather seats mixed with my mother's White Shoulders cologne. Dad had bought her a new bottle every year for their anniversary, for their entire married life. She held my left hand and Michael held my right.

The hearse passed another burial as we drove into the

cemetery. People milled about with handkerchiefs, many in hats, pods of mourners entwined in their grief. I felt tender toward them and wondered who they were burying; a parent, a sibling, a child? The word "death" was real now in a way it had never been; it had an entirely altered meaning to me.

Michael's arm was comforting on my shoulder as the casket was lowered into the gaping hole where my father would rest. I could hear the faint sound of a buzz saw somewhere in the distance, and then the whir of the lowering device drowned it out. The smell of the earth was overwhelming. I longed to leave this place and take a deep breath of fresh air that smelled of grass and sunlight. I hadn't run in more than a week and I burned to lace up my Nikes and do a ten-miler through the forest preserve. Or maybe a fifteen-miler. Or twenty. I wanted to run far away from this hole and the casket with my father inside and this new life that I'd have to live, without him.

Twenty

—ে৵৶—

Michael and I started planning our wedding right after the funeral. I was grateful to have a focus, something to fill my time and occupy my mind. There was so much to do, so many details to decide, so many places to visit, so many dresses to try on. I welcomed the busyness of it all. I felt my father watching me, knowing he'd have been happy, pleased that he wouldn't have to worry about me anymore.

Jill and Sophie were both alarmed at the shotgun speed with which our plans progressed.

"Why don't you slow down a bit, hon," Sophie suggested. "You don't have to rush it. It's not as if you're pregnant or anything."

Jill said, "It's too soon. Dad just died. Maybe you should give yourself some time to deal with that. There's lots of time to plan a wedding."

"It's okay," I told them. "I understand what you're saying but I'm all right. Dad would want this; he'd be glad I was going forward with it. And Michael's been so wonderful. I know he's the right man for me, the one I should spend my life with. It wasn't clear to me before, but it is now."

I had convinced myself completely, pushing my grief to a separate partition in my brain, and if Jill and Sophie weren't convinced, they were sure that I was. I was fifty years old, after all. So they both backed off and threw themselves into the spirit of planning, wanting to be supportive. Sometimes I think they should have tried harder to talk me out of it, but when I look back on that time I know that no one could have talked me out of anything.

Patrick e-mailed after the funeral with his condolences.

I know it's not easy. I lost my folks twenty years ago in a car accident. The hardest part was that they were here one day and gone the next. Just like that. Just ripped from my life without any warning.

My heart went out to him. I cried as I read.

You must feel something like that since your dad hadn't been sick or anything. I guess all we can do is be happy for the time we had with them and keep their memories in our hearts.

    My thoughts are with you, Libby.

    Love,

    Patrick

His words calmed me, as if he'd put his arms around me. It was comforting to know he understood what I was feeling. *Love, Patrick*, he had said.

    Patrick,

Thank you for your kind e-mail. It's horrible that you

lost both your parents at once, and in such a shocking way. It's unimaginable. I don't know how you would get through something like that.

Losing my father is the hardest thing I've ever been through. He's my hero and such a large part of my heart. I miss him so much. People keep telling me it will get easier but right now I don't see how. Now it is so raw and difficult and impossible, and I can't talk about him without crying. Wouldn't you think at 50 I'd be able to control myself?

Libby

A reply came back almost immediately.

Lib,

It doesn't matter how old you are—this is your father. Don't feel like you need to control yourself or keep from crying. You need to feel what you're feeling to work through it.

I went to a grief counselor when my folks died. I don't hardly tell anyone that—it seems such a wussy thing for a guy to do—but it really helped me. I tried for a while just to deal with it myself, but I have to tell you I just wasn't doing it. I'm sure there's something like that in Chicago. Maybe you could look into it. Death is a tough deal. I think the first time someone close to you dies it's sort of unreal and hard to get your mind around.

If you want to talk I'm here. Or you can call me just to cry if you want. If you need to do that, just do it.

Love,

Patrick

Ironically, for our wedding Michael and I decided on the Palmer House, the place where Patrick had stayed when he came to Chicago for our lunch date, the place where we made out at the bar.

We had considered the Drake, the Peninsula and the University Club but Michael and I both liked the Palmer House's Empire Room the best, the grandness and tradition of it. And it was available seven months from now on my father's birthday, which was the day we'd chosen. We would have a brief ceremony on the little balcony at the side of the room with a hundred or so guests gathered around, followed by an elegant reception with high-top tables scattered throughout the room.

"We can create an aisle that will lead from the double doors to the stage so you can make an entrance," Angela, the wedding coordinator, said. Tears filled my eyes when I envisioned walking down an aisle without my father. "Well, we don't have to have an aisle," she said as the tears streamed down my face.

"It's okay, sweetheart," Michael said, pulling me close. He explained about my father and Angela magically remembered an important errand that would only take her five or ten minutes, giving the weepy bride a chance to collect herself.

"It's okay," Michael said again when she'd gone, and handed me a handkerchief. "It's an emotional time, I know. Try to focus on the details and not concentrate on your dad not being there. He'll be there in spirit." I wiped my face and handed back his handkerchief, wondering briefly if he'd already blown his nose into it.

"Would you want my dad to walk you down the aisle?" he asked.

No, I wanted to scream, *I want my own father to walk me down the aisle!*

But Michael was just trying to help, so I said I'd think about it.

Twenty-one

—⁓ ❦ ⁓—

When Bea Rosatti came back from her cruise she called to see how I was. She needed some alterations done but assured me it was nothing she couldn't live without. "Whenever you're ready, dear," she said. "You just let me know."

"Thank you. But I need to work," I told her. "I can come by in the afternoon if that works for you."

"If you're sure. I have the whole afternoon free and a luscious chicken salad in the fridge. Come for lunch."

The chicken salad was luscious. It had grapes and almonds in it and she served it on nests of crisp lettuce with sliced tomatoes fanned out on the side of the plate.

"This is delicious," I said. "I want this recipe."

Bea's laugh was a bright, tinkling sound. "Okay, but you'll have to call Whole Foods and ask them because that's where I got it. I did slave over the lettuce beds, though." She wore a bright pink sweater with ruffles on the collar and sleeves, and matching pink dangling earrings. She looked like cotton candy.

"How is your mother doing?" she asked.

"She's okay. As well as can be expected, I suppose. She's a

strong lady. I stayed with her before the funeral. And a couple days after. But then she told me to go home." I swallowed. "I guess she didn't need me anymore." That was when I started to cry. All I did was cry these days. "I'm sorry," I said, using a napkin to mop my face.

"Don't be sorry. Cry." Bea put a box of tissues in front of me and poured sherry into small etched glasses. "It's not that she doesn't need you anymore, Libby, you know that. I'm sure she felt guilty that you were spending so much time with her. I'm sure she doesn't want to be a burden. And she probably feels she needs to be strong for you."

"But she doesn't," I said. "It helps me to be there for her."

"Just tell her that. Now it's especially important to talk to each other." I blew my nose. "Who's there for you, honey?" Bea asked.

"My mom. Jill. Michael."

"What's happening with Michael?"

"He's been wonderful. Very strong and supportive." Bea sipped her sherry, played with an earring. "We're going ahead with our wedding plans," I said. She raised an eyebrow. "We're getting married on my dad's birthday. In seven months."

"Well, that's lovely," she said.

"Yes, I'm happy. It took my dad's death to make me see how important Michael is to me." Bea handed me a tissue. I hadn't even noticed that tears were running down my face again. "I don't know what's wrong with me," I said and laughed. "I don't know why I'm crying. I'm happy."

"You're happy and you're sad."

I nodded. "I don't know what I feel anymore. Sometimes I feel like I can't function, like I can't think." A sob burst from my throat. "Sometimes I feel like I'm falling apart."

"Of course you do, Libby. Of course." Bea moved her chair close to mine and put her arm around me. She smelled of apples and spearmint. "It's a difficult time. It's hard to know if your emotions are real or if they're from grief. You just need to give yourself time. Don't expect too much from yourself."

I dried my eyes, downed my sherry and smiled. "Thanks, Bea." I stacked our plates. "I'm good now." She patted my shoulder and cleared the table. "Let's see what work you've got for me," I said.

She'd bought some things on the cruise: lime green capri pants with a navy and lime green jacket, a red dress with abstract splashes of white, all needing alterations.

"So how was the trip?" I asked as I pinned the jacket.

"Fabulous," she said. "I have pictures if you're interested."

"I'd love to see them." When I'd finished marking and pinning her clothes, we looked at a small stack of photos. They were large-format photos, professional ones taken by the ship's photographer.

"He was everywhere," Bea said, "snapping pictures at every opportunity, and then they were posted on a board the next day and everyone searched for theirs and exclaimed how expensive they were. And then they all bought every one of them. Just like we did."

There was the "Welcome Aboard" photo and the "Captain's Dinner" photo and then the disembarking photo at each port, Dominick and Bea waving to the camera as they stood on the gangplank. I went through the stack, occasionally asking for an explanation, oohing and aahing at a beautiful sunset or a long shot of the ship looking like a floating building. There was a photo of their dinner table, eight smiling faces, everyone dressed in elegant clothing, Bea in something short sleeved and red spangled. She and Dominick smiled at the camera while small red-haired children stood on each side of them, heads leaning on their shoulders. Behind them stood four adults, one obviously the mother of the children, a redhead with wide-set eyes. Bea was holding up her left hand, displaying a glinting ring.

"What's this?" I said.

"Oh, that," Bea said. "That's the night Dominick proposed."

My jaw dropped. "Proposed? Oh my god." I put down the pictures and hugged her. She felt very tiny. "I'm so happy for you. That's wonderful." I pulled back and looked at her radiant face. "I can't believe you kept quiet about this."

"It didn't seem like the right time," she said.

"Oh, it is. Truly. I'm so happy for you. Let me see that rock." I took her small hand. "How did I miss that?"

"You have other things on your mind," she said.

"It's beautiful." It was simple and elegant but quite large, and I thought about my own ring sitting in its box in my dresser drawer. I hadn't had it sized yet. Hadn't even taken it to the jeweler.

"Isn't this silly?" she said. "An engagement ring at eighty." But she was clearly delighted.

"It's not silly, it's lovely. Were you expecting this?" I asked.

"Not at all."

"Did he ask you in front of all these people?"

"Yes. Pretty sure of himself, wasn't he?"

I laughed. "I'll say. Very gutsy." I was thinking Michael had pretty much done the same kind of thing and it hadn't turned out so well for him. At least not at first.

"They all knew about it before I did," Bea said.

"You're kidding. Did you know these people before you went on the cruise?"

"No, they were just our tablemates, but it was the fourth night of the cruise and we'd all become fond of one another by that time. So he told them what he was planning and swore them to secrecy. They were nervous as cats, especially the little twins, but there'd been a chocolate tasting on the lido deck in the afternoon and I thought they were all just on a sugar rush."

"How did he ask you?"

"The waiter served me the ring on a silver tray with a lid. We all had trays with lids and the waiters stood behind us and lifted the lids simultaneously, and everyone but me had a lovely piece of fish. I had a small velvet box on my tray."

"How romantic."

"Yes, it was. And then Dominick took my hand and asked me to marry him and opened the little box to show me this beautiful ring. I cried and said yes, and then the entire dining room burst into applause." Her eyes flashed at the memory and she laughed.

"Oh my."

"And the photographer was snapping pictures all over the place and then some musicians came over and played 'Unforgettable,'" she said. "It was all terribly romantic."

"So how do you feel?" I didn't need to ask. Her face was like a display window into her delight.

"Like a schoolgirl," she said, and I felt a twinge of jealousy.

"I'm so happy for you. It's wonderful."

"Thank you, dear. I knew you'd be happy."

I remembered the day I had come to her house, when she and Dominick had been quiet and cautious with each other. It was the day Dominick had first mentioned the idea of their living together.

"It wasn't so long ago that you were unsure about moving in together," I said, "and now you're getting married. What changed your mind?"

"I think when Dominick first brought up the idea it just caught me off guard. But after we talked about it and I really considered it, it started to feel right, comfortable. And then I wondered why I *hadn't* considered it before.

"It's nice to think about having someone to spend my old age with," she said. "Not that I plan on being old."

"And you never will be," I said. "Well, it's wonderful, inspiring." We looked through the rest of the pictures. "My wedding gift to you will be your wedding outfit," I said. "You tell me exactly what you want—a dress, a suit, whatever—and I'll design it and make it for you."

"Oh, Libby, that's fabulous," she said, clapping her hands. "It'll be my honor to wear an original Libby for my wedding." *Original Libby.* I liked the way that sounded.

"Are you going to make your own dress for your wedding?" she asked.

"No," I said. "I thought I'd just buy one. Michael's going to help me pick it out."

"Michael!" she said. "Michael shouldn't help. Take your mom or your sister but not Michael. That's bad luck."

As I drove home I smiled at Bea's superstition. It was silly, really. It wasn't as if I were twenty, getting married for the first time, looking for a traditional white Cinderella-style wedding gown. What did it matter who helped me pick out the dress?

But then I thought that there was no point in pressing my luck; I decided I'd make an outing of it and ask my mom and Jill and Sophie instead.

Twenty-two

Libby,

I've been thinking about you and hope you're doing well. The weather's warm here and the sunset was beautiful last night. I had two kayak tours yesterday, one with 4 macho guys who were body-building, extreme-sports types, so I'm relaxing today. My 50-year-old body was pushed to the limit.

I found some information on grief counseling in the Chicago area and thought I'd pass it along. I hope you're not offended, I don't even know if this is right for you, I was just doing a little research and thought I'd let you know. Just in case.

He gave me phone numbers and web addresses for two options and signed his e-mail, *Love, Patrick*.

I wasn't sure I was ready for something like that, but felt as if he'd put a hand-knitted afghan around my shoulders. I looked at one of the counseling sites, for people who've suffered the loss of someone significant: a parent, sibling, spouse, child. It said that participants share their experience and learn about the grieving process. *Although grief is a normal human experience*, it said, *everyone experiences grief in his or her own way. Our group helps you cope with your loss and understand the feelings that come with change. We can help you regain your balance as you learn to accept your life in a new way.*

Balance would be good, I thought, and sat staring at the counselors' faces on the website: Rebecca, a thin, older woman with curly blond hair, and Henry, a gray-haired man with a kindly priestlike face and rimless glasses.

Patrick,

Thanks for the info. I'm not offended at all. It was sweet of you. I'm trying to get back on an even keel. It's not been easy but of course it's all still fresh and tender. I read one of the websites and am giving it some thought.

Michael and I are going ahead with our wedding plans. We're getting married on my father's birthday in seven months. My father would be very happy about this. Or maybe I should say he is very happy about it— who knows? I never believed in stuff like that before but I can't stand to think that he's just gone.

Libby

∿

I'd only known Michael a couple of weeks before I invited him to join me at my parents' house for dinner. This was an unprecedentedly bold and uncynical move for me so early in a relationship, but that's how right it had felt. I'd been on the phone with my mom one day, telling her how I'd met him, and there was apparently an uncharacteristic enthusiasm in my voice that perked her up.

"Well, Libby, he sounds delightful," she'd said. "Why don't

you bring your new boyfriend over for dinner on Sunday so we can meet him?" I hadn't even bristled at the word "boy-friend."

She'd gone all out, as if entertaining the monarchy. You'd have thought I was a forty-year-old spinster with a face full of unfortunate moles, wearing elastic-waisted pants and orthopedic shoes.

Lamb chops glistened juicily on each plate, surrounded by brightly colored al dente vegetables with an artfully arranged sprig of parsley on the side. She'd set the table with her Irish lace tablecloth, linen napkins and china, and created a centerpiece with a single gardenia floating in a glass bowl surrounded by votive candles. Martha Stewart had nothing on my mother.

Michael smiled approvingly at the plate before him.

"I can't remember the last time I had lamb chops," he said.

Actually, we'd had them over the weekend at Ditka's. I caught his eye and smiled, hoping it wasn't early-onset Alzheimer's.

"What business are you in?" my father asked.

"Real estate," Michael told him, and they were off and running with the do-you-know conversation, since my father was a real-estate attorney. It seemed they had a lot of acquaintances in common and mutual opinions of them all, if Michael were to be believed. After the lamb chop comment I wasn't sure, but he acted very sincere, and he and my father were bonding. I was pleased.

My father's fine, white hair was neatly combed and he wore a mustache that had changed from black to white in my lifetime. Age spots spattered the slackened skin of his hands, which shook faintly as he cut his meat. But he was always in motion, my dad: reading, gardening, golfing, working on the computer. My mother diagnosed it as ADD.

"Libby's got a great little business going," Michael said when they'd exhausted the directory of real-estate personnel in the greater Chicagoland area. "It's quite a success story, I'd say, leaving a successful corporate job to start something new. That's a pretty gutsy thing to do."

He beamed at me. I chafed at my parents' isn't-that-wonderful smiles, feeling as if I were twelve instead of fifty, but in spite of myself a blush rose from my chest under Michael's admiring gaze, as if the teacher had just given me a gold star.

"The lamb chops are great, Mom," I said.

"Yes, delicious meal, Kathryn," Michael said, pushing his wire-rimmed glasses up onto the bridge of his nose. "You should have a show on the Food Network. You could call it *Cooking with Kathryn.*" When he smiled, lines pleated the corners of his soft brown eyes.

"How about *Dinner to Die For?*" I said.

"Or *Kathryn's Kuisine*, with a *K*," my father said.

"Oh, you guys," my mother said. Her cheeks were rosy with pleasure. A hint of blue eye shadow tinted her lids, and her pearl earrings matched her necklace.

"More lamb, dear?" she asked my father.

"How am I going to keep my girlish figure if I have seconds?" he said, as he always did. "But this is the best lamb you've ever made."

I smiled at this exchange, the predictability of it.

"It's the best lamb I've ever had," Michael said. "I'll have more, if you don't mind."

She popped right up and put two more chops on his plate.

The way to my mother's heart: ask for seconds.

Mom and I cleared the table as Michael and Dad got into an enthusiastic discussion about the '85 Bears, another shared passion, it seemed.

"The Bears were the most dominant team in football that year," my dad had said.

"If they'd beaten Miami they would have had a perfect record," Michael responded.

"Who was your favorite player from that team?" my father was asking as Mom and I carried plates to the kitchen.

I started lining up dishes in the dishwasher while Mom decorated individual pavlovas with fresh strawberries and hand-whipped cream.

"He's adorable," she said.

"He is, isn't he?" I prized the way he fit in.

"Dad gave me a thumbs-up," she said and I laughed.

"I didn't see that."

"Well, he didn't do it so you could see it, silly. But it's obvious he likes him." She poured coffee into her sterling silver carafe, which I hadn't seen since Jimmy Carter's presidency. Was she going to offer a dowry, too?

"Do you think you have a future with him?" she asked.

Normally, here's how this conversation would have gone: "Jeez, Mom, relax, I hardly know the guy."

Mom: "Well, you have to consider these things."

Me: "I'll consider it after I find out his last name and make sure he's not on the sex-offender registry."

Mom: "Oh, I'm sure he's not." Said with no irony. "I think he's a good man."

Me: "You've known him for twelve minutes. They're all good men for twelve minutes. Let's give it at least an hour. I'll get back to you on that."

But that day I said, "Maybe," in a high-pitched, girly voice followed by an appalling giggle, and Mom's eyes had danced with happiness.

Fast-forward to another dinner, not even a year later—chili

and cornbread served on everyday china and plastic place-mats.

"Do you think you and Michael have a future together?" she'd asked as she scraped dishes into the sink.

"This *is* our future, Mom."

Little did I know.

"Men like him don't grow on trees," she said. "I just think you should consider it."

"He's not going anywhere. We're good."

"Well, just don't expect him to be perfect," she said. "At your age you need to be able to compromise."

"What does that mean? And what makes you think I don't compromise?"

"I'm not saying you don't compromise *some*. But at your age, people are more set in their ways."

I stopped loading the dishwasher. "Jeez, Mom, quit saying 'at your age,' would you? I'm not *that* old. I don't even have an AARP card yet."

"I know, I know. But you're not getting any younger. And it's not that easy to find a good man, especially at your age." I set down a cup. Hard. She looked up. "Sorry. I just mean that you're not a teenager anymore. And fairy tales are for children."

"You think I'm expecting life to be a fairy tale? That train left the station some years ago, don't you think?" I rinsed a few more dishes. "Are you afraid I'm going to chase Michael away with my demands of perfection?" She didn't respond. I watched her as she cut large hunks of lemon meringue pie and lifted them onto small blue plates. "I'm not expecting a fairy tale, Mom," I said.

"Just accept that Michael's human, honey. And that there are no perfect people."

What the hell? "I don't expect people to be perfect." She

didn't argue, but the air was heavy with her opinion. "I guess I missed the rule book that tells you how to act when you get to be *my age*."

"There's no need for sarcasm," she said and I felt rebuked, just as if I were twelve. "I just want you to be happy."

"Yes, me, too."

"Pour the coffee, would you please?" Conversation over.

The pie had three inches of pearly white meringue that was browned lightly on the waves and swirls. We carried it with the coffee into the dining room, where the men were once again doing an '85 Bears postmortem. It was their tradition by now.

"Hmmm, talking about the Bears for a change?" I said, and three heads turned to me as if choreographed. I looked at each one and laughed. "What?" I said. "Just thinking we could talk about something else."

"Well, okay," my father said, "let's talk about when you two are going to get married."

"Dad! Jesus. What is this, an intervention?"

"Don't you think it's time?" he asked.

I looked at Michael, who was not only unfazed but was unsuccessfully attempting to suppress a smile. I cocked my head at him.

"Did you put him up to this?"

He laughed. "Don't look at me. I'm an innocent bystander here." He forked another piece of pie into his mouth.

"Nobody put me up to anything," my father said. "It's just a reasonable question."

"How is it I still have to answer questions like this at *my age*?" I looked at my mom but she ignored me.

"Because you're still my little girl," my father said. "No matter how old you are. So why not get married? You've been together for, what? Five years?"

"One," I said. "Not even. But we're not twenty-year-olds, Dad. And it's not like we're going to have kids. I'm in my forties, remember?" I was forty-nine. "And Michael's pushing sixty—"

"Fifty-eight," Michael interjected.

"I know very well how old you two are," my dad said. He looked at Michael. "Well, I didn't realize you were sixty."

"Fifty-eight," Michael said.

"Well, anyway, I know you're not going to have babies, but why not get married?"

"Michael," I said. "Would you please tell them we're happy the way we are?"

He looked up, fork poised over his plate. "We're happy the way we are."

"I'll tell you what," I said to my dad. "When Michael and I decide to get married, you'll be the first to know."

"Well, good," he said, and that seemed to be the end of it.

I'd taken a big bite from the large slice of pie in front of me but now there was a mist of silence hovering over the room. I looked around the table. Then my dad had said, "Do you think it'll happen before I die?"

I'd wondered when I'd stop feeling like a teenager at my parents' dinner table. I remembered sitting at that very table thirty-five years before, answering my father's questions about who I was hanging out with, where I was going, what college I should go to.

It seemed as if nothing had changed, except that I was ten pounds heavier and my hair had a forest of silver threads running through it. Oh, and then there were those fucking hot flashes. A trade-off, I guess, for no longer having pimples. But if I had to pick the lesser of two evils, I couldn't do it.

Twenty-three

It turned out the new Michael wasn't finished with surprises. He called one afternoon to see if I was available for a little field trip. "I have something I want to show you," he said. "I'll be over in half an hour."

He wouldn't respond to my questions. Each "Where are we going?" was met with a mischievous smile. When he finally did answer, his voice held a little kid's excitement. "You'll see in a second," he said.

He drove down Marshall Street and then made a quick left on Cherry, where my favorite house sat proudly with the FOR SALE sign out front. Only now there was a bright red SOLD sticker on it. I looked at Michael. His eyes were shining and a smile was ready to explode off his face.

"I made an offer on it."

I heard the words but they didn't compute. "What do you mean, you made an offer on it?"

"Just what I said, I made an offer on it."

"You're kidding."

"Nope."

"Wow." What else was there to say?

"My offer was accepted," he said.

Now I was dumbfounded. "You *bought* it?"

"Yes. Can you believe it?" The car was too small to contain his excitement. "You always said whoever lived in that house would just have to be happy."

"But Michael, I have a house."

"I know, but that's *your* house, not *ours*. This old couple lives here. They've been here since they got married. They're so cute. When I told them about how you always loved this house, they were so excited."

His eyes shone. He was so eager and proud, about another fucking surprise.

"How did this happen?" I asked, making an effort to keep my voice even and calm.

"I was looking at the new listings and when I saw that your favorite house was on the market, I called the listing agent. We went right over and made them an offer and they accepted it. It all happened so fast."

I sighed. "Oh, Michael." A garden gnome watched me carefully from the neatly trimmed shrubs. "What if I don't want to live here? What if I don't want to sell my house?"

"Why wouldn't you want to live here? You love this house."

"I love it from the outside. I love to run by it, sure. I love to imagine what it's like. But Michael! What if it's not what I imagine?"

Michael laughed. "Let me assure you it's not. It definitely needs work. But we'll make it whatever you want it to be. I got a really good deal on it. We can live in your house while we remodel this one. And then we can sell your house and move in here." *Sell my house?* All these plans, he had it all figured out. It made my temples pound.

He moved close and put his arm around me. "Come on, you can go see it."

I gazed out the window, not trusting myself to talk, agitation bubbling up inside like an oil well. I was torn between wanting to run screaming from the car and the overwhelming desire to finally see my dream house.

He reached for the door handle. "Ready?"

"We can't just go inside," I said.

"It's okay, hon, they won't mind. I told them we might be by this afternoon. They're expecting us. They're anxious to meet you."

Fear, excitement, distress, gratitude all swirled through my head like dust devils. But I got out of the car anyway and we walked up to the door. White rockers sat on the porch and for a moment I got a pleasant little picture of us having a glass of wine out here on a warm evening. We were old in this fantasy, and Michael wore a gray cardigan. I was old, too, but my hair looked great, pulled up in a little bun with soft tendrils falling around my face. Very Katharine Hepburn–ish.

It was *my* fantasy, after all.

And then I saw the Stroms, who looked as if they were blood related in the way of people who've been together most of their lives; both ample, with big open faces and wide smiles showing even, beige teeth. Their bulldog hung just behind them looking up at Michael and me with the same expression. He could've been their offspring.

"Oh Libby, so nice to meet you," Mrs. Strom trilled, grasping my hand. "Michael told us so much about you."

"It's nice to meet you, too," I said.

We stood in the entryway. Ahead of us was a wide stairway to the second floor, the living room to the right and the dining room to the left. On the floor where we stood was olive green shag carpeting that looked as though it had been there since it was trendy in the sixties. There was a bentwood coatrack against one wall and a large blue and white urn on the other, filled with a rainbow of plastic zinnias, thickly coated with dust. The walls were covered in faded green and gold wallpaper.

"Come in. Would you like something to drink?" Mr. Strom asked, leading the way into the kitchen. "Mother forgot to do the breakfast dishes," he observed. He patted his wife's shoulder and clucked his tongue. I thought if the dishes had all been from that morning they must have had guests, perhaps the front line of the Chicago Bears. There were dirty pans on the stove, and the sink was piled high with plates and glassware. I doubted there were clean glasses in the cupboards. No matter. After seeing this, the probability that I would accept anything to drink or eat from this house was as likely as finding a Jacuzzi in their marble bathroom.

"No, thank you," Michael and I said in unison.

"Well, so this is the kitchen," Mrs. Strom said. "There's lots of cupboard space." A layer of grime varnished every surface. With her cane she walked slowly around the room opening cupboards. Her thick bowlegs looked painful to walk on. Mr. Strom helped her along, sweetly gripping her arm.

"We ate our meals right here in this very room for sixty years," she said, indicating a chrome table with a Formica top. The chairs had thick brown vinyl seats with duct tape patches.

This house did not fit into my *Father Knows Best* fantasy, although it probably had some of the same furnishings. "Vintage" was how Michael, as a Realtor, would describe it. "Gut-job" would be my description.

"Great space, isn't it?" Michael said. "This is such a great kitchen." I forced a cough to cover the hysteria bubbling up in my throat. The Stroms beamed at him as I pictured a wrecking ball going to work on the walls and appliances. By now I had seen as much as I wanted to see. If I got out now I could preserve a little part of my fantasy.

No such luck.

"Let's go this way. The dining room's right through there," Mr. Strom said, as his wife tottered sluggishly, leading the way.

By the time we had worked our way upstairs and were peering into the only bathroom, I was nearly delirious with revulsion. Brown one-inch tiles paved the bathroom floor and climbed halfway up the walls. Worn, dark paneling covered the rest. A tiny sink was set into a vanity that was yellowed white with brown trim. The counter was made of fake marble. Also dark brown. Two people could occupy that bathroom at the same time only if they were conjoined twins.

"Well," I said brightly, "thank you so much for your hospitality, but we really must be going."

"Oh, it's our pleasure, dear," Mrs. Strom said. "We're so happy you all bought it. Can you stay for tea and cookies? I made oatmeal raisin cookies yesterday. Papa's favorite."

Mr. Strom nodded happily. "They're the best," he said. "Mother missed her calling. I always told her she should have packaged them and sold them. We could have been billionaires."

"That's very kind of you," I said. "But we have an appointment we need to get to."

Michael smiled at them and grasped their hands warmly. "Thanks so much," he said. "This is a great house. I'm very excited."

At the door, when we were finally close to our escape, Mrs. Strom said to me, "I know you'll be very happy here. It's a happy house."

Michael smiled as we drove back to my house, my clean, neat, updated house with its hardwood floors and granite countertops and unsoiled walls. "It has great bones, doesn't it?" he said.

"Bones are all it has," I said. "It would cost a fortune to make that place livable, Michael."

"Well, yeah, it'll cost some bucks. But don't you think it's like fate that it went up for sale now? It's like it's meant to be, you know?"

"Well, you know I'm not a believer in stuff like that," I said, "but I admit the timing is impressive." He laughed, smug with happiness, which made me want to slap him.

I did the next best thing.

"Enough with the fucking surprises, already," I said. "I don't understand this, Michael, really. You can't keep doing this, making decisions for us as if I don't even count. We need to make these kinds of decisions together. I've had enough surprises to last me a lifetime."

He flinched and looked at me with wounded eyes. "Jesus, Libby, I thought it would make you happy."

"Buying me a bouquet of daisies would make me happy, or a pralines-and-cream gelato. But a *house*? How do you make an offer on a house without even mentioning it to me? We've got to both be invested in this, don't you see that? You need to stop thinking you know what will make me happy and start talking to me. Especially about something this huge. Do you understand what I'm saying?"

"I have a contract on it," he said.

"Jesus, Michael, what's with the strong-arm tactics? I understand that. But you acted impulsively and it may not have been the best decision." He grunted. "No more surprises, Michael. Promise me. You need to save the surprises for the small stuff, not for houses."

He sighed.

"Promise me, Michael."

"All right, I promise," he said, and we drove the rest of the way home in silence.

Twenty-four

⟶◦ ✷ ◦⟵

Early in my relationship with Michael we had been so in synch. We remarked on the same odd things at the same time, liked the same foods and books and furniture. We even finished each other's sentences. It had been reassuring and enthralling to feel so connected to someone, like two birds sitting on the same perch. Now something had shifted in me. I attributed it to my father's death and the new reality I was living in. Lately, Michael's and my perspectives seemed uncommonly divergent. I had this feeling that I was black and white, living in Michael's Technicolor world. But I didn't trust my judgment, unconvinced that I hadn't done or said something to encourage his uncharacteristic behavior. It was certainly true that I'd remarked on that house every time we passed it, always making wistful comments about what it would be like to live there. Why wouldn't he feel sure I'd be thrilled with his surprise?

So I let my irritation melt away and turned my thoughts to kitchen cabinets, natural stone countertops and greenhouse windows.

I didn't know if I'd continue to hear from Patrick after telling him about my wedding plans, but he seemed unfazed. I didn't tell Michael about the correspondence but I didn't feel guilty—it was just e-mail, after all, and it always gave me a good, warm feeling when I saw his screen name in my in-box.

Libby,

I'm happy for you and Michael. He's a lucky guy. How are the wedding plans coming along? Is it going to be a big blowout affair?

How are you doing? How are you feeling? Have you looked into grief counseling? I don't mean to be pushy, just curious. One of the things it gave me was a place where I could talk about my parents and no one would tell me I should think about something else. That helped me a lot. Also, another thing I thought was a really good idea was writing a letter to the person who died. They said it helps you understand your feelings and is a way to say things you can't say in person anymore. I'm not much of a writer but it was good for me.

Love,

Patrick

I loved the idea of writing a letter to my dad. There were so many things I wanted to share with him. I could see how it might bring me comfort. I had never before believed in an afterlife, but now I couldn't bear the thought that he wasn't in some way still out there, a spirit or an essence that could communicate with me somehow. If I wrote a letter maybe my words would reach him.

Patrick, I wrote back,

Always nice to hear from you. I'm doing okay. Good days, bad days . . . you know. I like the idea of a letter to my father. I'll try that sometime.

I do really appreciate your suggestions and I don't feel like you're nagging or anything. Some people seem to think I should move on, get over it. But it's hard. It makes me feel like I have to put up a front so other people won't be upset. That's fucked up, don't you think? I hope I never did that to anyone who was mourning a loved one.

Michael and I are having a small wedding, about 80 people. A judge will marry us in a very brief ceremony and then there'll be a cocktail party following. Heavy hors d'oeuvres and cocktails, that kind of thing. My mom will walk with me down the aisle.

Michael bought a house and didn't tell me. It's a house I've always loved in the neighborhood and it came up for sale and he put in an offer to surprise me (Michael's a Realtor, did I tell you that?), and his offer was accepted. My head's spinning. The house is a mess. Needs billions of dollars in renovations. But it'll be perfect when we're finished. It has a great porch.

Jill and I are going to a bereavement group, one of the ones you told me about. I'm nervous. We both are. Nervous, anxious, scared. But there's also a little relief in it.

Write me soon.
Libby

🐦

The room was decorated in soothing shades of forest green and burgundy, one wall lined with bookshelves with plants and snow globes among the books. Comfy chairs were placed in a semicircle in front of a fireplace and two women were already seated, sipping coffee from bright yellow mugs, talking quietly when Jill and I walked in. They looked up and smiled. It was all very warm and welcoming, homey. I burst into tears.

A man came toward us, hand outstretched, tissue box in hand. "Welcome," he said. "I'm Henry." I recognized him from his picture on the website. He was taller than I expected, heavier, a little older. His silver hair was cut very short and he wore a plaid shirt under a cardigan. "Don't worry," he said as I wiped my face. "It happens to a lot of people."

We introduced ourselves and then he introduced us to the two women, Carlyn and Lisa, and offered us coffee. People drifted in while we stirred cream and sugar into our mugs. My stomach churned. I didn't know what to expect. I guess I had thought everyone would be sobbing into shredded tissues, but these people all seemed calm to me, peaceful.

"You okay?" Jill asked.

"I don't know. You?"

"I don't know," she said. "I'm not sure I want to talk about how I feel with a bunch of strangers."

"Me either. But I'm sure we don't have to say anything if we don't want to," I told her. I wasn't really sure of anything.

The session began with everyone introducing themselves, just names and why we were here. There were eight of us, two men and six women—four who'd lost parents, two who'd lost spouses, one who'd lost an aunt, and Carlyn, who'd lost a three-year-old child. She told her story dry eyed, but sorrow embossed her face, and I wiped my own tears as she spoke.

When we were finished Henry said, "There is no greater stress to the human system than death. Everyone grieves differently, and no one's loss is greater or lesser than anyone else's." I was sure the death of a three-year-old trumped all of our losses. "Sometimes when we suffer a great loss we lose our perspective, our sense of self-worth. We question our reasons to go on. But as trite as it sounds, life does goes on, and healing comes when you reach out and embrace your own life.

"Mourning is hard work. It's exhausting. It can feel as if every little action requires superhuman strength. But we'll do it a step at a time. Don't move too fast at first. Don't expect too much of yourself. And don't let anyone else tell you how to grieve."

My spine softened, my shoulders relaxed a bit. I leaned back into my chair.

"For the time we're together we're going to be kind to each other, and patient. We're going to help each other. This is a safe place where you can talk and cry and gain strength. It's a place where you'll learn that it's okay to laugh again. In here we'll learn to live the rest of our lives in a new way."

❧

Jill and I were both tired as we drove home. "That wasn't bad," she said.

"No. It was good. Even though I cried the whole time."

"You're a cryer. Always have been."

"Yeah. You'd think I'd outgrow that."

"There's still time," Jill said. "You're only fifty."

"I hope it happens soon. There's no percentage in crying when you're over fifty. It takes forever now for the swelling to go down."

The night was cool and clear. I opened my window a crack to let fresh air blow on my puffy eyes. I liked the feel of my hair blowing off my face. "I think it helps to be with people who know what you're feeling," I said.

"I wish we could have talked Mom into coming with us."

"It's not her thing," I said. "She belongs to the Church of

Don't Talk About It and It'll Go Away. They both did. Dad always told me to turn the other cheek, especially about men. He thought you should just keep quiet and accept things. 'Keep your counsel,' he always said. He never saw the good in talking things through."

"I know. It's the time they grew up in. People weren't so open in their generation."

"How do you and Mark resolve your differences? Do you guys talk a lot?" How was it I'd never asked her this before? Maybe all this time she'd been holding the key to a successful long-term relationship.

"He ignores me, I pout," she said. "We move on."

The streets were serene as we got closer to my house. "Remember that house on Cherry Street?" I said. "The one with the white picket fence?"

"The *Father Knows Best* house? I love that house."

"Michael bought it for us."

"You're kidding," Jill said, looking at me, eyebrows raised. After a beat she said, "That's so cool. I didn't even know you were looking for a house."

"I didn't either. He did it on his own. Didn't even mention it to me until it was a done deal."

She turned to me, then back at the road. "Libby, what the fuck?"

"I know. I know."

"You can't do that when you're a couple. Part of being married is working together, having common goals." She was more indignant than I would have thought, and it made me feel defensive of Michael.

"Calm down, Jill. It's not that bad. He knows I love that house. He wanted to surprise me."

"You don't surprise someone with a *house*, for Christ's sake. It's not like a new toaster. Jesus. What if you didn't like it?"

"But I did like it. He knew that."

I couldn't bring myself to describe it or tell her how much it was going to cost to remodel. I regretted telling her about it at all. Her reaction made me clamp my mouth closed and I glared out the window, craving quiet.

"Still . . ." she said. I blocked her out.

We rode in blessed silence for a while. She avoided Cherry Street, driving down Maple instead, three blocks out of our way. When she pulled in front of my house I said, "Thanks for driving," and started to open my door. Jill put the car in park and turned to me. "Don't go yet, Lib, I want to say something."

No, don't, I thought, but sat back and waited. Her face was serious in the half light from the streetlamp. She looked like she had at four years old when she told me our dog had died while I was at school—the same frown, the same penetrating look in her eyes.

"In the spirit of being open," she said, "and not being an ignore-it-and-it'll-go-away kind of person . . ." She smiled. I didn't. "You know what Henry said about not making big life changes after a major loss? Remember? He said we shouldn't make any important decisions until our lives feel more on track?"

"I remember," I said, looking at my garage, wishing for the door to rise and suck me inside.

"You're doing it in spades, Libby. Getting married, moving, selling your house . . . it's a lot. You're like the poster child for what not to do."

"Michael and I were already engaged. Before."

"But you weren't sure you were going to marry him. Remember that? You were questioning the whole thing. Then Dad dies"—the words were still shocking—"and all of a sudden you're sure. It's not a decision that was already made."

Tears rolled from my eyes. She took my hand. "I'm not saying don't do it, you know that, don't you? I'm just saying wait a little while."

I took my hand away, shook my head. "I can't."

"Why not?"

Because Dad wants me to be married, I almost said. "We already have the Empire Room booked, we bought the invitations, we hired a photographer." I put my hand on the door.

"Listen to me, Libby, please." The oak in the front yard whispered with the breeze. The shelter of my house beckoned, a soft light in the den window.

"I love you. I want you to be happy. If you want to marry Michael, then that's what I want for you. But I don't think this is the right time to make these kinds of decisions. Sometimes now it's hard for me to decide whether to scramble my eggs or fry them. I find myself standing in the kitchen not even knowing what I was going to do"—her voice broke—"and I'm just consumed with the fact that Dad's not here anymore and I'll never be able to talk to him again. It kills me. It just kills me."

Jill buried her face in her hands and made small sounds that broke my heart. I scooted over and put my arms around her. "I know, baby, me too," I said. We sat like that for a while, crying for what we had lost, the void that we were facing. My sister was the only one who truly knew how I felt.

When we quieted I moved back over to my side of the car. I said, "I think Dad would be happy about me marrying Michael."

Jill studied her perfect manicure, bit at an imaginary hangnail. "I'm not sure, Lib," she said.

My eyes welled up. Again. As if I hadn't cried enough today. My face will be swollen for weeks, I thought.

"God, don't say that," I said. "You're making me crazy.

One minute you tell me to marry Michael and the next you tell me not to." I opened my door.

"Lib," she said, grabbing my arm. "I'm sorry. This whole thing with the house just worries me. It's so extreme. I just want to be sure you're marrying Michael for the right reasons and that you're not being pressured, that's all."

"I know. I appreciate your concern, really I do," I said. "But I know what I'm doing." She didn't look convinced. "I'm going in now. I just can't talk anymore tonight. I'm on overload."

Jill's eyes were dark with dejection. My little sister.

She said, "Whatever you decide, I'll support you. I'll be there for you; I'll do whatever you want me to do. I love you, Libby. You're my soul. I want you to be happy."

I dug in my purse for a tissue and blew my nose. I saw the little girl she used to be, the messy little tomboy, the one I cried with when I was five and she was three and she skinned her knees when she fell playing hopscotch, and I felt her pain in my own knees. She was at the very core of me.

I said, "I have a stomachache all the time. I can't sleep. I miss him so much. I feel like there's a hole in me."

"I do, too," she said.

"But Dad didn't worry about you the way he worried about me. You're married. That was the difference. He wanted that for me. Michael has a lot of the same qualities as Dad. He's a good, kind man who'll take care of me. And I feel like he can fill that emptiness for me. How can that be bad?"

"It's not bad. It's good. The thing is, no one can fill the emptiness that Dad's left. You have to learn how to live with it. We both do. And we will. It just takes time. All I'm saying is, keep things simple for a while and then figure out where Michael fits."

I sighed. I yawned, hugely. "I can't talk anymore, Jill. I can't think. I'm exhausted. I'm done. I'm going in. Now."

I wanted to climb into bed, pull the covers over my head and sleep until I didn't feel like this any longer.

"I'll call you tomorrow," she said. "I'll support whatever decision you make, I promise. I love you, Lib."

"I love you, too, sweetie," I said, and hugged her to me before getting out.

I couldn't get away fast enough.

Twenty-five

❧ ✦ ❧

Dear Daddy, I wrote that night when I woke at 2:30 A.M. and couldn't go back to sleep.

I miss you so much. I've never believed in an afterlife but I can't bear the thought that you are just gone. I need to feel that you're still with me. Sometimes I feel you watching me. But I want something tangible. I want a sign.

Tonight I had a dream that I was transporting your body somewhere, I don't know where. I knew you were dead but you were sitting in a chair, a wheelchair-type thing with a high back. You reached up and rubbed your nose. I stared at you for a minute and then I said, "Daddy, are you okay?" and you said, "My nose itches," and I said, "But you're dead," and you said, "I know."

We talked for a while, I don't know what about, and then I said, "I wish you weren't dead," and you said, "I know you do, honey, but it's really better this way. I'm okay." I said, "I love you so much, Dad," and you said, "I love you, too, honey." And then I woke up. I cried a little

but really, I feel sort of peaceful cuz you said you were
okay.

　　Was that my sign?
　　I love you,
　　Libby

I sat at my desk waiting for my answer. The house was still. Rufus was still asleep on my bed. The furnace purred, the refrigerator hummed, I heard a siren far off in the distance. If any of that was a sign, it was too subtle for me.

I didn't feel sleepy enough to go back to bed so I went to my computer, where I was pleased to see an e-mail from Patrick. It was like sunlight seeping inside, embracing me.

Libby,

　　How'd the session go? I hope it was worthwhile. And not too tough. I remember the first one I went to, I didn't think I'd go back—all those people sitting around emoting was a little much for me—but the next day I felt calmer. So I did go back. And I'm glad I did. It was a good thing for me.

　　I have to tell you this, Lib, and that is that I'm worried about you. One thing I remember from the group I went to—the woman who led it said we shouldn't make any big decisions in our lives for at least a year. That keeps going through my mind. I've hesitated saying anything because I don't want to piss you off by butting in where I don't belong. I've been going back and forth, having conversations with you in my mind, and I decided that since I'm your friend I'm just going to tell you what I'm thinking and you can ignore it if you want.

Getting married is a big change. I know you and Michael have been together for a while, but still . . . you live separately, and even though you're a couple you're still single. So I'm just bringing it up as something for you to think about. I'm not recommending anything one way or the other, I just want you to think about the decisions you're making now and be sure you're not rushing into something out of your grief and a need to put things in some kind of order. I think the kicker for me was the house thing. Wow. That sort of freaked me out.

So there it is. I hope you're not upset by my words. I promise I won't mention it again.

Love,
Patrick

What the hell was with everybody? Why did my decision seem so right to me while people all around me saw it so differently? I wasn't angry with Patrick for saying what he did. But I didn't answer him either. I did add a P.S. to the letter to my father, though.

Here's what I need to know, Dad: You're happy I'm marrying Michael, right?

I went to the kitchen and poured myself a glass of Pinot Grigio. I looked into it and studied it for several moments. For what? My dad's face reflecting back at me? Maybe a big "Yes" or "No" written in clouds on the surface? But it was just wine. So I took it to the living room, curled up on the couch with the afghan and contemplated the fact that I was past middle age, practically a senior citizen, and still felt like a lost child.

Twenty-six

—୧ ❦ ୨—

Libby,

I haven't heard from you in a while and just want to make sure everything's okay. I hope you're not upset about what I said. I didn't mean to imply you shouldn't get married. I'm not involved in your life—I don't see you regularly, so what I said was meant to be taken with a grain of salt, okay? If you think now is a good time to be married, if you're happy about the house, then I am, too. You're a big girl and I'm sure you know what you're doing.

How is everything going? How are you feeling these days?

It's so great being in touch with Pete and Sophie. I talked to Pete on the phone the other day for about an hour. They're thinking of making a trip down here, did they tell you? Sometime after their daughter's wedding. Maybe you could come with them. With Michael, of

course. I have a big house, room for everyone, not far
from the beach.

E me.

Love,

Patrick

Did he really think that was a possibility? I could just
imagine Michael's response to that idea. I laughed at the image in my head of Michael and Patrick meeting in the hallway, towels wrapped around their waists, toothbrushes in
hand. I could see us all in pajamas and fuzzy slippers making breakfast, like a scene from *The Big Chill* only without
the dancing. It had been a long time since I'd traveled with
Sophie and Pete, and if it weren't so impossible, it would
have been fun. An opinion Michael surely wouldn't share.

I hadn't answered Patrick's last e-mail. He was entitled to
his opinion (no matter how misguided it was), but it had
irked me. I don't like being told I'm making a mistake when
I'm so sure of what I'm doing. Never have. But I thought
about what he'd said and couldn't help wondering if he had
my best interests at heart or if there was a hidden agenda in
his words. My ego would have liked equal shares of each.
And then, of course, there was that *Love, Patrick* at the end
of every e-mail that gave me a golden glow every time I read
it, even though I never wrote it back.

Patrick,

I'm not upset with you. I do appreciate your concern and am giving consideration to your words. I realize you're not trying to tell me what to do, just telling
me what you think, and that's fine.

I'm doing okay. Life goes on, as they say, but the
pain doesn't go away. I guess you just learn to live with

it, although that's not happening so quickly either. The bereavement group is a big help to me and to my sister, so thank you for telling me about that. There's something comforting about being with people who know what you're going through.

I wrote a letter to my dad as you suggested. In fact, I've written a couple. I like doing it—it makes me feel that he's close. Unfortunately he's not answering my questions, but I'm thinking he's putting the answers out there in the universe somewhere for me to find them. He always encouraged my independence, so why start making it easy for me now?

I'm glad you and Pete have rekindled your friendship. It still sort of amazes me to be in touch with you after all these years. I can't imagine Michael and me coming to Florida with Sophie and Pete. It's such a funny idea. Not that it wouldn't be fun. But thanks for the invitation. I hope S and P make it, tho.

Libby

🐏

"I thought I was going to help you pick out your dress," Michael said when I told him I was going shopping with the triumvirate: my mother, Jill and Sophie. I regarded him as he put on one black sock, then a shoe, then reached for his other sock.

"Why don't you put both socks on first, then your shoes?" I asked.

He looked at his bare foot, then at me. "I don't know. I've always done it this way."

"I know. I've always thought it was weird. What if there was a fire? You'd be running out in the street with one bare foot."

He laughed and shook his head. "Talk about weird," he said, and put on his other sock and shoe. "So how come I'm not shopping with you?"

"Don't you know it's bad luck for the groom to see the dress before the wedding?"

"It's probably worse luck for the bride to wear a dress the groom doesn't like."

"You think I'll pick out something you wouldn't like? You always like what I wear." Michael watched his reflection as he tied a red striped tie over his blue shirt. "Don't you?" I asked.

"Sure," he said. "I just thought it would be fun to do together. That 'bad luck' thing is for kids—the Cinderella fantasy. I think we're a little beyond that, don't you?"

"Yes, several hot flashes beyond that, but we're also beyond engagement rings and weddings and we're still doing those."

He cocked his head at me. "Touché."

Michael was spending more and more time at my house. He seemed to be moving in by centimeters—a pair of socks in the laundry basket, jockey shorts in a drawer, more pants hanging in the closet. We hadn't talked about it, it was just happening. It's hard now to imagine that I just went along with it, but at the time I didn't have the energy for the confrontation a discussion would surely cause. Besides, he was my fiancé. What was there to discuss?

"Maybe you could take a picture with your cell phone and send it to me before you buy anything," he said.

"Maybe you could just wait and be surprised," I said. He pulled the tie apart, apparently not satisfied, and started re-knotting it.

"You never used to be so controlling," I told him.

He met my eyes in the mirror. "Controlling?"

"Yes, controlling."

"How so?"

"*How so?* Let me count the ways."

"Hmmm. Okay then, don't send a picture and I'll be surprised," he said, and finished knotting his tie.

❦

I stood on a pedestal in front of a trifold mirror, swathed in fluffy silk organza while the bridal consultant and my mother oohed and aahed. Sophie and Jill both wore expressions that said, *Oh, please.*

"You look like you're twenty years old in that," my mom said.

"Yeah, if you don't look at my fifty-year-old face."

"You're *fifty?*" Cara, the bridal consultant, said with such incredulity that I wanted to hug her and buy the damn dress. "I thought you were in your thirties." Bless her lying little heart.

If Jill was still concerned about me marrying Michael now and making so many life changes, she hid it well and got into the spirit of the day, moving from rack to rack, offering up various options. Ultimately we'd all picked out four dresses—the big puffy thing being my mother's choice, of course—and I was the human mannequin.

"It's a bit much, Mom. I know you love this style but this wedding is going to be more like a fancy cocktail party with a marriage ceremony thrown in. Did you pick out anything less frou-frou?"

"No," she said. "But humor me and try them on anyway." So I did, while Jill yawned and Sophie filed her nails.

Sophie's and Jill's choices ran more toward Nancy Reagan: elegant suits and conservative tea-length dresses. Mine leaned in the direction of Cher: a slinky black beaded dress with a silver shawl, a knee-length burgundy silk skirt and sequined top, a low-cut red evening gown with fringed jacket.

By the time I finished trying on the last option we were all worn out and I was no closer to buying a dress than I'd been when we walked in. I could only imagine what we looked like to Cara: three middle-aged women and a senior citizen, slouched in our chairs, bags under our eyes, hair disheveled. She wore a little half smile as she rehung the last of the dresses. "I'm going to go get you each a glass of wine," she said, and we all perked up. "And then I'm going to bring one last dress for you to try on." I groaned. "I know," she said, "but I think it may be just what you're looking for." How could she know? She was twelve. But what was one more dress? Besides, I really wanted that wine.

We sat in exhausted silence, sipping our wine and nibbling on the cookies she'd brought, until Sophie said, "Pete talked to Patrick the other day and invited him to come to Danielle's wedding."

I stopped chewing. Patrick, here? At Danielle's wedding? Patrick and Michael in the same room? "Why'd he do that?"

"He's just so happy to be in touch with him. It's like he has a new best friend." She turned to Jill. "Patrick Harrison," she said. "Remember him?"

"I do," Jill said with raised eyebrows. "What rock did he crawl out from under?"

"The Internet," I said.

"Well, well," Jill said. "Things keep getting curiouser and curiouser."

"Anyway," Sophie said, "Pete wants to get together with him and they were talking and I think it just came out." She shrugged. "I think he might come."

I swallowed.

"Who's Patrick?" my mother asked.

"Libby's high school boyfriend," Jill said. "Remember the guy with the long hair and the black leather that you and Daddy hated?"

"Oh, I'm sure that's not true," my mother said. "We never hated anyone Libby dated."

Jill and Sophie and I laughed. "Well, okay, maybe 'hate' is extreme, but you weren't crazy about his long hair," I said. "Do you remember him?"

"Oh honey, I barely remember you. How could I remember someone you dated in high school?"

"Remember the Bradshaws?" Jill asked. I gave her a look but she kept going. "Remember when Libby went to a New Year's Eve party at their house?"

"No, dear, I don't remember. And I'm not going to tax my brain. But what's the difference? It's all ancient history." She looked at me. "Have you kept in touch with him?"

"Just recently we got in touch through a website where people find their high school friends."

"SearchForSchoolmates.com?" my mother asked.

I almost dropped my wineglass. "How do you know about that?"

"Do you think I sit around and knit all day?" she said. "I'm the technology queen of my book club. I've taught everyone how to use a computer. I've been on that website a number of times. Although as you can imagine there aren't many of my classmates left."

My mother on SearchForSchoolmates.com. Amazing. What if she was e-mailing old boyfriends?

"Who'd you find?" Sophie asked, clearly delighted with the idea.

"I found a girl I used to run around with, Sarah Posen."

"Does she live here in Chicago?"

"No, in Michigan. Not too far, though. We're going to try

to get together soon. I'd love to see her. Haven't laid eyes on her in about sixty years."

"Technology is amazing, isn't it?" Jill said.

"It is," I said. "How would we have gotten in touch with these people years ago? It would have taken so much effort that no one would have ever bothered. Now it's as simple as having a computer and an Internet connection, and you can get reacquainted with someone you haven't seen in sixty years."

"Or thirty," Sophie said.

Cara came back with an elegant ankle-length crocheted tank dress and matching jacket in a shimmery bronze color. It was shot through with metallic shine and there were tiers of scalloped lace at the hem. We all nodded when we saw it, our heads bobbing, smiles on our faces. It was perfect. I had a wedding dress.

Twenty-seven

❧ ❦ ☙

The next two weeks were a blur of activity. There were long stretches of time when I just spaced out, couldn't think what I was doing or where I was going, and then I'd come to, because I had to pay attention to Michael's details and all his various plans.

He decided to sell his condo and in two days had a contract with a coworker who'd often expressed interest in it. Why was everything happening so fast? First the *Father Knows Best* house and now this. It was as if Michael had a golden touch.

He wasn't closing for eight weeks but he'd already started packing and bringing things to my house box by box—kitchen things, picture albums, books, things I had no room or use for. The boxes went straight to the basement for storage, stacked up like little condos in a corner.

He called an architect and we had meetings to discuss renovations on the new house, even though it wouldn't be ours for two months. Everything was moving at warp speed and I went along, swept up in the whirlpool of activity.

I worked with Bea Rosatti on her wedding outfit, which

was to be a fitted, knee-length dress with long sleeves and a V-neck, and a jacket with a ruffle down the front and on the sleeves. I'd sketched out several options for her and she'd surprised me by picking the most conservative one. But my elegant, dignified design morphed into something very Bea-like when she picked a silky, sparkly, watermelon-colored fabric that was like water to work with.

And during those weeks, the two weeks before Danielle's wedding, Patrick and I exchanged e-mails about his upcoming trip to Chicago. He was excited to see Sophie and Pete again and to meet their daughters. He was happy he would be seeing me, which warmed my heart, and he was looking forward to meeting Michael. At least that's what he said.

Michael was less than thrilled.

"That's ridiculous," he said. "Why would Pete invite him? He hasn't seen him since high school."

"I suppose that's why," I said. "He's happy to be in touch with him again."

"If he wanted to be in touch with him so badly, why didn't he make an effort all these years?"

Michael's tone exasperated me. I had no desire to have a conversation about it so I left the room, went to my workroom and picked up Bea's dress, cut out the facings, pinned them to the armholes. Pretty soon Michael was standing in the doorway. I pretended not to notice.

"He's just coming because he wants to see you," he said. I almost grinned. When I didn't reply Michael said, "How do you feel about it?"

I looked up from my work, peering at him over my reading glasses. "I feel fine about it. It'll be nice to see him again so soon."

"So soon?"

Oops. I'd forgotten that Michael didn't know Patrick had

come to Chicago to have lunch with me. It seemed so long ago now.

So I told him.

"You're kidding," he said when I'd finished.

"I'm not," I said, concentrating on my pinning.

"Wait, let me get this straight. He flew, what, a thousand miles to have lunch with you."

"That's right." Inside it gave me a little chill.

I could feel Michael's eyes on me but I just continued my work, one pin after the other.

"What's with this guy? Does he have his own plane?"

"He's a little impulsive," I said.

"A *little*?"

I stabbed my finger and a small red bubble rose up. "Ouch. Goddamn it." I sucked on it and squelched the urge to tell Michael to shut up and get out. So what if Patrick was impulsive? What the hell did it matter? I put down the fabric, took off my glasses and looked at him, finger in my mouth.

"Let it go, Michael." I said it as quietly as I could manage.

"I can't," he said. "I hate this guy and I don't want him here."

I laughed out loud. Not because I was amused but because Michael sounded like a ten-year-old instead of a man nearing sixty. I imagined him throwing himself to the floor, kicking his legs, face about to explode.

"You don't even know him. And anyway, it's not up to you. Pete invited him and he's coming. He's just a guy, Michael."

Michael narrowed his eyes. "There's no such thing as *just a guy*," he said.

"You're jealous," I said.

"I'm not jealous. I just think the whole thing's stupid."

"Well, fine, think it's stupid. It is what it is and you're going to have to deal with it, and it would be nice if you'd act like a grown-up about it." He stared, eyes blazing. I could see all the retorts bubbling up behind his lips, which were locked in a tight line, and braced myself.

He turned.

"I'm marrying *you*, Michael," I said to his rigid back as he walked away. "I bought a dress!"

Twenty-eight

❦

The day of Danielle's wedding might have been ordered from a catalog titled *Weather for All Occasions: Birthday Weather, Funeral Weather, Wedding Weather.* The skies couldn't have been bluer, the clouds puffier, the sunshine shinier. And the white church was dazzling with its stained-glass windows and spire reaching to the heavens. Everything was perfect. It was a fairy tale, that Cinderella wedding Michael and I were too old for.

"Psssst." Tiffany's delicate face peeked out the vestibule door. She was flushed, and I could see lots of lively purple behind her as the bridesmaids bustled around the room. She grinned and waved, and I heard giggling as she shut the door. Michael and I smiled at each other and headed into the church.

"Bride's side or groom's?" the usher asked. He was young and handsome, in a black tuxedo with a purple cummerbund and bow tie, dark hair gleaming with styling gel.

"Bride's," I said. He offered his arm and walked me down the aisle with Michael following. The organist played something soft and sleepy as we took our seats. I looked around at the expectant faces, scanning the pews for Patrick, but I didn't see him. I worked to squash the disappointment bubbling up.

When the music stopped, the murmuring of voices ceased, processional music began, clothing rustled as people turned in anticipation. First came Sophie's parents, looking vibrant and healthy, then Pete's mom, frail but bright with pleasure. The groom's mother and father came next and then Sophie, elegant in a champagne-colored suit with a peplum waist and ankle-length skirt.

The poofy purple confections came next, three bridesmaids with their respective groomsmen, and then Tiffany. Gone was the punked-out kid with spiky orange hair and pierced eyebrow. In her place was a graceful and composed young woman, her hair a conventional shade of dark blond, tucked behind her ears and swept off her face in soft waves. Aside from the swarm of earrings trailing up her left ear, she was understated. She made the dress look classic and lovely. No hint of a giant iris.

"The dresses are great," Michael whispered, and I puffed up with pride.

The regal blast of trumpets sounded then: *ba ba ba bum, ba ba ba bum . . .* and Mendelssohn's "Wedding March" began. A little girl in a pink dress stood on the pew in front of us, craning her neck to see. Her eyes sparkled and she jiggled up and down, barely able to contain her excitement. I smiled at her and she clasped her little hands together, her mouth forming a perfect O.

Then the doors at the back of the church opened dramatically and Danielle and Pete stood silhouetted against the sunshine outside. They began their graceful walk down the aisle, Pete's face aglow with pride.

How many years ago was it that Sophie walked down the aisle in that same dress? Too many to even comprehend, but

I could see it as if it were yesterday, watching from the altar in my coveted spot as maid of honor. It brought a lump to my throat.

My dress had been baby blue with an appliquéd bodice, hyped as something I could wear again and again. Of course I never had. It had taken its place in my bridesmaid's hall of fame. But Sophie's dress had made the transition beautifully. It looked flawless on Danielle, as if it had been made for her. I hoped wearing it was an auspicious beginning, that her marriage would be as strong as her parents'.

As Danielle and Chris recited their vows I choked up again: "I will be yours in times of plenty and in times of want, in times of sickness and in times of health. . . . I promise to cherish and respect you, to care and protect you, to comfort and encourage you, and stay with you, for all eternity."

What is it about weddings, I wondered, that makes us cry? The sweetness? The sentimentality? The failure rate?

All eternity? Whew, that was a long time.

❦

By the time we got to the reception my tears were long forgotten. We'd had a couple of hours between the ceremony and the reception so I'd suggested to Michael that we stop for a drink.

"Don't you think we'll be drinking enough at the reception?" he'd said.

"Absolutely not," I said. "And anyway, that's hours from now. What else are we going to do? Go *bowling*?"

"Bowling," he said. "Hmmm . . ."

I swatted at him. We stopped for a glass of wine.

Mark, Jill and my mother were sitting at a large round table with a lavender lace tablecloth and iris centerpiece when Michael and I arrived. Pete's sister Stacy and her husband, Fletcher, were there as well. And there was one empty chair, which made my heart ache. I worked hard at swallowing the lump it brought. It was times like these that snuck up on me and threatened my footing. Sophie had told me she put Patrick in that seat and I wished he were there now. I wished someone was, just so it wouldn't be so heartbreakingly vacant.

But no Patrick. Had he changed his mind?

A three-piece combo played chamber music as guests mingled and found their seats, and after a while the violinist took the microphone to announce the wedding party. They streamed in: the groom's parents, Pete and Sophie, the brides-maids and ushers. Tiffany was last with the groom's brother, her new beau. They made a cute couple. He was a few years older than Tiffany, maybe seventeen or eighteen, tall and lanky, handsome in his tux, smiling from ear to ear. He guided them into a little twirl as they entered the room and Tiffany giggled, putting her hand to her mouth. I could see love in her eyes.

Then the big announcement: "And now," drum roll, "for the very first time, I have the honor of introducing . . . *Mr. and Mrs. Christopher Sanderson.*" The bride and groom walked in, smiles illuminating their faces. Danielle blushed with all the attention but gazed adoringly at her new husband. I felt melancholy watching them. I would never be in their shoes again, getting married for the first time, feeling that new love, the promise it held.

Michael put his arm around me. "That'll be us before long," he murmured.

Not like that, I thought.

We were into our salads of roasted beets, arugula and blue cheese when I looked up and saw Patrick and Pete heading toward our table, and my spirits rose like Old Faithful. I put down my fork and swallowed, hard. Pete wore a delighted grin. "Here he is," he said when they got to us. "Finally. Can you believe it?"

Patrick's hair was a little longer than when I had last seen him. He looked so handsome it made my throat dry. His smile was wide as he caught my eye, and I felt a flush start at my chest and work its way up.

"Sorry, all," he said. "My flight was delayed."

He came right over and kissed my cheek. Michael sat up and stared, a lion sizing up its prey.

"Great to see you," Patrick said, squeezing my shoulder. When he took his hand away I still felt its imprint. "You must be the famous fiancé," he said to Michael, shaking his hand.

"Guilty as charged," Michael said.

"You're a lucky man."

"Yes, I am." He smiled. "Finally we meet," he said. "I've heard a lot about you." I was surprised by his words, his equanimity. No one would ever guess the snit he had been in about this man.

Patrick moved around the table, greeting everyone, charming them, including my mother.

"You haven't changed a bit," he told her.

"Well, that's the nicest lie I've heard in a long time," she said. "I can't say the same for you, but that's because I don't remember you. It's a wonder, though."

He smiled. Then touched her arm. "I'm so sorry about your husband." Her eyes shone with gratitude.

He kissed Jill and Stacy. Stacy grinned hugely. She'd had a crush on him when we were young. "Look at you," she said. "Still handsome."

"Look at you," he said. "Pete's little sis. Still gorgeous." Stacy laughed loudly. She was at least forty pounds heavier than she'd been in high school.

"A bit bigger than the last time you saw me."

"Who isn't?" Patrick said. "You look great." He shook Fletcher's hand. "Nice to meet you," he said, and then sat in the empty chair and everyone picked up their forks. Jill gave me a look across the table. Clearly he'd lived up to whatever expectations she'd had.

♥

"Next week is our anniversary," Stacy announced as we ate our Dover sole. "We've been married twenty-four years."

"Congrats," Patrick said.

"Lovely," my mother said.

"Jill and Mark have been married, what? Twenty-six years? Twenty-seven?" I said.

"Twenty-eight," Jill said.

"How did that happen?" I asked. "How'd we get so old?"

"Just lucky," Patrick said.

"Lots of marriage longevity here," Stacy said. "Good karma for a wedding."

"I'm skewing the karma," I said. "Maybe I should find another table, the one for the longevity challenged."

"Not to worry," Michael said. "Your record's about to change."

Stacy raised her glass. "Yes," she said, "congratulations, you two." We all clinked glasses. Patrick caught my eye for a moment but I couldn't read his expression.

I said, "May this marriage be my longest one ever."

"May this marriage be your best one ever," Michael said.

"And your last," my mother said.

We all drank.

I could barely remember my first two marriages, at least not the day-to-dayness of them—they were a very long time ago, in another life. But I clearly remembered the unraveling, strand by miserable strand. One thing was sure—it was certainly less complicated being single. There was no one telling you you were doing something wrong, no one hogging the bathroom, no one to cook for or clean up after, no one who left lights on and drawers open. You didn't have to compromise with your own self.

I hadn't always been so cynical. There was a time when the fairy tale had been alive and well, when I thought I'd live happily ever after with the love of my life, my soul mate. The first one came in the form of husband number one, who was elegantly handsome with a generous spirit. He adored me and made me feel beautiful, and we "walked off into the sunset" of our tiny apartment to live the dream, which we did for about two years until the novelty of having sex for breakfast, lunch and dinner wore off and it became evident that we had nothing else in common. We didn't laugh at the same jokes or like the same movies. He liked to camp; I liked spas. It was amazing, really, when I woke up to that reality.

Still, when the marriage failed I was astonished. I never thought I would be a divorced person. I was flattened. But once I recovered from the affliction of my failure I was undaunted, figuring I'd simply picked the wrong Mr. Right and the right one was still out there waiting.

Husband number two turned out to be another wrong Mr. Right.

I stopped looking for a soul mate after that. It seemed a little like looking for Santa Claus—a lovely, make-believe concept. It was ridiculous to think that someone's soul could cleave to your own, or that you even needed that. Now I was a grown-up and more realistic, wanting a partner, a confidante, a best friend, someone to have fun with, be comfortable with and grow old with. With some passion thrown in. And Michael fit that bill. Mostly.

I wasn't 100 percent sold on the whole concept of marriage in general anymore, yet here I was about to try again. Was that hopefulness or folly? Or equal shares of each? Around me, the conversation had continued. "Married men live longer than single men," Fletcher said. "Did you know that?"

"Yeah, yeah, we know, but they're a lot more willing to die," Stacy said.

They seemed solid and happy, touching each other occasionally, feeding each other tastes of their food, and they'd been together a long time. But how do you really know what goes on in a relationship?

Patrick turned to my mom. "What's the secret of a long, happy marriage?"

"Oh, well," she said, a little flustered. "I guess I'd say compromise, patience, luck." She looked around at the expectant faces. "Empathy, respect. That all helps," she added and sat back.

"Laughter," Jill said.

"A husband who doesn't snore." Stacy.

"A great pot roast." Mark.

"Agreeing with everything your wife says." Fletcher.

"Oh yeah, as if you practice that," Stacy said.

"I do," he said.

"Do not."

"Do, too," he said and then, "Oh, oops, I mean yes, dear, you're right." Stacy laughed, slapping at him.

"An endless supply of vodka is a plus," Mark said.

Michael leaned toward me and said, "I hope you're taking notes."

"I don't have to. I'm already well stocked on vodka."

Tuxedoed waiters cleared our plates and refilled our wine. The violinist played something indistinct in the background.

Patrick said, "I sat next to a couple on the plane who bickered the whole way up here: he hadn't packed the right clothes, she should have gotten her mom to stay with the kids, why didn't he tell the flight attendant she wanted extra ice, they should have gotten a suite . . . that kind of thing. God, it was painful. And then when we were landing they told me they were going on an Alaskan cruise to celebrate their fifteenth anniversary." He shook his head. "Hard to know what makes a marriage work."

Michael said, "I think being with the right person is the key. Maybe that couple on the plane likes to argue, maybe it energizes them, who knows? But if you're with the right person, you just mesh in whatever way works for you. It may not look ideal from the outside, but that's not for us to say." His tone was a little pompous, as if he were some big marital guru.

Patrick didn't seem to notice.

"Amen," he said.

"Well, if you want the secrets of an unsuccessful marriage, I'm your girl," I said.

"Then here are the secrets to a successful one," Jill said. "Don't do what you did before."

"She's not. She's marrying me," Mr. Matrimony said.

Wasn't there something else to talk about at a wedding besides marriage? I wondered what Patrick was thinking, what he thought about me and Michael as a couple. And I wondered if this truly would be my longest, and last, marriage.

The band announced the bride and groom's first dance and the couple floated out on the dance floor as the guests applauded. I felt inspired and moved by their shimmer. Christopher took Danielle in his arms as the band played "Can You Feel the Love Tonight." His face was set in concentration and you could almost hear him counting his steps for the first few moments, but Danielle followed effortlessly. Then Pete cut in, taking his daughter in his arms, and Chris went to dance with his mother. We all watched until the band invited everyone to join them. Stacy grabbed Fletcher's hand. "Come on," she said, waving us all forward. I always had to plead to get Michael to dance with me, so imagine my surprise when he popped right up and guided me to the dance floor, leaving Patrick and my mother behind. I watched them over Michael's shoulder, deep in conversation, heads bent toward each other. I fantasized that Patrick was telling my mother that he intended to steal me away from Michael.

"Nice wedding," Michael said, vaporizing the imaginary conversation in my head.

"Mmmm-hmmm."

"Good food. We should find out what caterer they used."

"Why?" I asked, watching Patrick lead my mother to the dance floor. She rested her hand on his shoulder and smiled, shaking her head. Patrick took her other hand and they moved, slowly.

"Duh . . ." Michael said, like a fifteen-year-old girl. "For our wedding."

The song ended and the band went into "Celebration." The older people who hadn't had the requisite amount of liquor left the floor and the rest of the younger people poured onto it. Michael shook his head and shrugged, cutting his eyes toward our table. His dancing skills, such as they were, were limited to slow dances, rhythm not being one of Michael's strong suits.

"Look at you!" Stacy said delightedly to Fletcher who was doing some fancy footwork as Michael and I walked away. Fletcher took Stacy's hand and spun her around, and she threw her head back and laughed. It was nice, I thought, when you could be surprised and enchanted by someone you'd been married to forever.

My mother and Patrick were still dancing, too slowly for the music, and as we got close to them she threw up her hands and said, "No more," and latched on to Michael's arm.

"Stay and dance," Patrick said to me. Michael looked at him. "Do you mind?" Patrick asked him, without a trace of irony.

Michael hesitated only briefly before he said, "Of course not," and ushered my mom to the table.

The music thumped loudly as Patrick and I danced through several songs, waves of nostalgia washing over me. The former Patrick and Libby danced in my mind, young and strong and in love. Patrick's eyes flashed as if he were seeing the same image.

When the band started playing "Hot Hot Hot," he said, "Come on," put my hands on his waist and started a conga line. Soon a long procession filled in behind us and we snaked around the room while Michael sat drinking beer. When we passed him I put out my hand for him to join in but he shook his head and we slithered on by.

Sweat dripped down the back of my dress and frizzed my hair. When the band went into "Philadelphia Freedom," a song we'd danced to in high school, Patrick and I grinned at each other.

"Whew," he shouted over the music, "I haven't danced like this in years. Maybe since this song was new." His hair was damp on his neck and his crisp shirt was wilting, but his neon smile made something bloom inside me.

"Okay, *uncle*," he said when the song ended. He put up his hands as if he were under arrest. "I need a break, babe."

Babe.

He guided me to the table with a hand on my back. "Thanks for the loan of your fiancée," he said to Michael. "She about wore me out."

Michael glanced at him, then took a swig of his beer. "You two ought to try out for *Dancing with the Stars*," he said.

"Oh, I love that show," my mother said. "But those dresses the girls wear are so revealing."

I laughed at my mother and ignored Michael, who obviously had more than a few beers under his belt.

Pete came to the table waving a box of cigars. "Come on, guys," he said. "Time for a cigar and brandy in the bar."

"Cool," Patrick said and got up, but Michael didn't move.

"Come on, Michael," Pete said.

"Nah," Michael said.

"Come on, man. It's male-bonding time. Let's go get Fletch and Mark off the dance floor before they keel over."

"Yeah, let's go save them with cigars and liquor," Michael said, and reluctantly got up.

"I don't think Michael needs brandy," my mother said when they'd gone.

"He doesn't need a cigar either, but I suspect he'll do both."

"He's not very happy about Patrick being here."

"I know. What do you think of him?"

"Patrick? He's charming, of course. I have no memory of him from your high school days."

"You probably blocked it," I said. "Dad would have, too. Back then Patrick was kind of a tough kid with long hair, and you know how Daddy felt about long hair on boys."

"Well, he certainly turned out well, didn't he?" She smiled.

"Yes," I said. "He certainly did. You think Daddy'd like him today?"

"Oh, I think so."

I pulled my hair up in back and wiped my neck with a napkin.

"Daddy was crazy about Michael," I said.

"Daddy liked him a lot," she said, but something in her tone raised my eyebrows.

"That didn't sound very convincing."

"Oh, honey," she said. "Michael's a good man. And he's never been afraid to show how much he loves you. Your father liked that. And he liked how responsible Michael is. He was glad you finally found someone stable and kind. He didn't like to think about you being alone."

I could picture the pleasure on his face when we announced our engagement and it made my eyes sting. I wished he were there with us, talking.

"I hear a 'but,' " I said.

My mom scanned the room, likely looking for someone to come rescue her. When no one appeared, she picked up a fork and took a tiny bite of a miniature cream puff we'd gotten from the dessert buffet. "Have some," she said.

"No thanks." I waited patiently. Well, maybe not so patiently. I crossed my legs and swung my foot like a metronome, and ran my finger around and around the rim of my wineglass. I wanted to know and yet I didn't. Dread settled inside me. It seemed she was going to say a terrible thing.

"Libby, settle down," she said.

"Come on, Mom. Just say it. It's starting to feel like something really awful."

I stuck my finger in the cream puff and licked a bit of custard off of it, just for something to do.

"Oh, it's not awful. For heaven's sake. But sometimes it just doesn't matter what route you take when you're going to the fair, it just matters that you get there. Do you know what I mean?"

"The *fair?*" I said.

"What I'm trying to say is, I'm not sure it was Michael as much as *someone.*"

Someone? As in *anyone?* As in a warm body?

I peered at her but she watched the dance floor intently, fingering her napkin. I waved at a waiter and he came scurrying over and topped me off. I took a swallow, put down the glass and waited. She knew I was looking at her.

Sophie saved her by returning to the table with a plate laden with petit fours, tiny éclairs and shot glasses filled with pillows of chocolate mousse. "Look what I scavenged for us," she said, flopping down in an empty chair and spooning up some of the frothy mousse. "So what are you two talking about?"

Jill was right behind with her own plate overflowing with chocolate-covered fruits.

"Mom just dropped a huge bomb on me," I said.

"Oh, honey, I didn't."

"You certainly did."

"What?" Jill said.

"All this time I thought Daddy thought Michael was my Mr. Right, and Mom just told me he didn't."

"Oh, Libby, that's not what I said." My mother crumpled her napkin and dropped it on the table. "He liked Michael, I told you that. Did he think he was Mr. Right? I don't know. But he thought he was right enough."

"Right enough? What the hell is *right enough*? If he walks upright and doesn't drool, is that right enough?"

Jill laughed. "Right enough's not such a terrible thing," she said.

Easy for Miss Perfect to say.

"It sounds terrible to me," I said. "It sounds like I'm such a loser that I should just marry whoever will have me." A *loser?* Even I could hardly believe what I was saying. But it felt as if my beloved father had been disappointed in me and now I'd never have the chance to make it up to him. Unbelievably, tears welled up in my eyes.

"No more wine for you," my mother said. Sophie laughed, and I glared at her until she stuffed a large hunk of chocolate-covered apricot into her mouth.

"Have one," she said around the mass. "Delicious." The word came out like "delithoth."

I reached up to stop a tear from making a track through my makeup.

Jill plucked my wineglass and moved it out of reach. "Okay, really, enough wine, enough crazy talk. Honestly, Libby—what more do you want? So what if Dad didn't think Michael was Mr. Right? Since when did that ever matter to you?" She looked at Mom. "Right?" Mom nodded, a scrap of a smile wafting around her lips.

Sophie said, "Did you ask his permission to date Patrick? And that guy with the purple hearse . . . what was his name?"

"Vincent," my mother said, causing us to swivel our heads and stare in stunned silence. "Well," she said, looking around, "he reminded me of Vincent Price, and that car just reinforced it."

We all laughed. "*I* didn't even remember his name," I said. But Sophie was right; my father'd had no use for him and it had mattered not a whit to me.

"And how about that guy who looked like George Chakiris?" Jill said. "Daddy just *loved* him." She rolled her eyes. "And weren't you *engaged* to him?"

"Okay, enough," I said. "We'll be here all night if you're going to go through the entire list."

"We'd need a database for that," Sophie said, "and I left my computer at home."

198 ᴄ Samantha Hoffman

She looked radiant. Her hair was freshly highlighted and cut the way she'd worn it in high school, short and casual. She looked the same to me. Ageless.

"All right, all right," I said. "I get the point." The tension in my neck was loosening ever so slightly.

"Libby," Mom said. "Daddy just wanted you to be happy. He thought people weren't meant to be alone, that's all. You know how he felt about you. You were the apple of his eye." She remembered Jill then, and patted her hand. "Both of you," she said.

"I was no apple. Libby was the apple," Jill said. "I was the egg."

"The *egg* of his eye?" I said and started laughing. Jill laughed, too. Then Mom started, and Sophie, and pretty soon people were watching us, unable to keep smiles off their own faces. Each peal of laughter caused another and it bounced around the table, and we couldn't stop for several minutes; every time we looked at each other we'd start up again, until we were all wiping tears from our eyes.

What an odd evening this had turned out to be: my mother telling me my father didn't care who I married as long as I married; my fiancé and my high school sweetheart somewhere smoking and drinking together, saying who knew what to each other.

The tide of my emotion had subsided but I felt disoriented, as if I had just realized the bus I was on was going in the wrong direction. It was true I'd never before required my father's seal of approval for any man I was with, from the time I was young. I'd never lived my life the way my father thought I should, but even if my decisions had troubled him he always encouraged my independence. Didn't he always tell me to follow my heart, whether it was about a man or a career or where to go on vacation? So why did I have this idea now that I should live a life he had engineered? Did I think that then the hollowness inside would go away?

Michael and Patrick came back to the table fogged in cigar smoke. Patrick was in high spirits, Michael not so much, but no worse than he'd been earlier. I don't know what I'd expected. Evidence of a fistfight? A black eye?

"So have you all bonded?" my mother asked.

"You smell like you have," I said.

Patrick laughed. "Just like Krazy Glue," he said. His cell phone rang then. "Oh, sorry, I thought I turned it off." He checked the display and said, "Excuse me, I need to take this," and wandered away speaking in low tones. Who was it? Who was so important that he had to answer the call in the middle of a wedding reception?

"Come on, Lib. Time to go," Michael said. "Let's go say our goodbyes."

"Oh, let's stay a bit longer," I said. "There are people I haven't even talked to yet."

And I haven't found out who Patrick's talking to, I thought.

"Your mother's tired," he said, "I told her we'd take her home." I looked at her.

"I'm fine if you want to stay a bit longer," she said, but now I could see the weariness around her eyes. Still, I didn't want to leave. I wanted to dance with Patrick some more and laugh and reminisce about old times. I saw him now on the dance floor with Sophie and couldn't take my eyes off them, heads together, talking earnestly. When they both threw back their heads to laugh at something I wanted to run out there and say, "What? What? What's so funny?" And to find out who he'd been talking to.

"How about just half an hour?" I said.

"That's fine," my mother said.

"I want to go now," Michael said.

It occurred to me that Michael could leave and take my mother with him and I could get a ride home later with Pete and Sophie. Or with Patrick. But Michael's face was set, his arms were crossed and he stood looking at me as if ready for a fight. If not for my mother's presence I might have pushed it. But I didn't want to make a scene. I'd acted like a spoiled child enough for one night so I agreed to leave, though I wasn't happy about it.

We said our goodbyes to the bride and groom, then to Tiffany, who said, "No, you can't leave yet!" and Pete, who said, "Leaving so soon? The party's just getting started."

"Michael's had enough," I said.

Michael bristled. "Kathryn's tired," he said.

"It's way past my bedtime," my mother agreed, ever the peacemaker.

"Oh, I have a feeling you could out-party us all," Pete told her. "Hey, are you all coming for brunch tomorrow?" I hadn't planned on it—it was for the out-of-towners—but now that Patrick was here I perked up. "Absolutely," I said.

"I'm not sure," Michael said. "I might have a showing tomorrow."

I was sure he had no showing but didn't care if he did or not.

We stopped on the dance floor to say good night to Sophie, who was still dancing with Patrick. He shook Michael's hand. "It was great meeting you," he said.

"Yeah," Michael said.

Patrick kissed my mother and told her it was good to see her looking so well after all these years. She hugged him warmly. Then he gave me a peck on the cheek and said, "It was wonderful to see you, Lib." I glowed inside. I wanted to hug him but I didn't.

"You'll come to brunch tomorrow, right?" Sophie asked. "You, too, Kathryn."

"We will," I said at the same time Michael said, "We'll see." I felt Michael look at me. I said to Sophie, "Well, *I'll* be there."

"Good," Patrick said.

I smiled at him and gave Sophie a hug. "It was a fabulous wedding," I said, feeling happier now. "Really fabulous."

Twenty-nine

❧ ❧ ❧

When I walked my mother to the door she took both my hands and said, "I shouldn't have said what I did about Daddy just wanting you to be married," she said. "It sounded bad. He liked Michael very much. He thought he was a good man, that he made you happy. We both did." Damage done, I thought. "Promise me you won't do anything rash."

"Rash? Like what?" I said.

"Like anything," she said. "I can see what kind of mood you're in. Just think things through before you make any decisions."

"Should I pick you up for brunch tomorrow?"

"I wouldn't miss it for the world," she said. I laughed, and was still smiling when I got back in the car.

"What's so funny?" Michael asked.

"Nothing," I said.

He backed out of the driveway and headed for home.

"Do you really have a showing in the morning?"

"No," he said. "I just don't want to see any more of that guy."

"Did something happen when you all were smoking your cigars?"

"No. I just think he's an asshole."

"Michael!"

"Well, he shows up out of the blue and stirs things up. I just think it was inappropriate," he said.

"Oh, Michael, you sound like an old fart."

We drove the rest of the way in resolute silence, exasperation simmering inside me. What had attracted me most about Michael in the beginning was how compatible we had been, how in step. There were times when we expressed the same thought simultaneously, or said, "I was just going to say that!" with such delight. Neither of us had been hesitant about what we wanted or what direction we were going, and we fell into our relationship easily, like sliding into a warm pond. We'd begun with the basics—attraction, chemistry, a shared sense of humor—and we kept adding our experiences and conversations and goals until we had a sturdy and familiar history.

Those good feelings were still there, somewhere in the background, but the memories were like puffs of smoke. I wanted to feel that way again. Oh, I knew I would eventually—I know all about the tides of relationships—but that knowledge was of no comfort. The arguments we'd been having recently weighed on me. I thought they probably weren't all that unusual for people like us, who'd been self-contained for so long and were now adjusting to this impending collaborative reality. But couldn't Michael see that I was still reeling from losing my father, that I just needed him to wrap his arms around me and kiss the top of my head and be sweet to me? Don't people sometimes set their own grievances aside, if only for a short time, just because the other person needs them to?

We were getting ready for bed when Michael said, "I'm not going to that brunch tomorrow."

"Big surprise," I said.

"And I don't want you to go either."

I turned to him. His chest was bare and vulnerable in the low bedroom light. My fingers paused at the button on my blouse. "Well, I'm going."

His eyes darkened. "I wish you wouldn't, Libby."

"I'm sorry if it bothers you," I said, "but I'm going."

Michael pulled on his pajama top, buttoned it slowly, watching me. "Do you care how I feel?" he asked.

"I care, Michael, but it's irrational." A flush crept up his neck. "It's your problem, not mine. It's a few hours with Pete and Sophie—"

"—and Patrick."

"And Patrick."

"Your former boyfriend."

"It's a few hours and then he's going back to Florida. And everything here will be just the same as it was before."

"Will it, Libby?"

"Why wouldn't it be?" I asked.

"I don't know. You tell me."

Just let me be, I thought. Tell me to go and have fun, that you're just worried, even if it's irrational, but that our life together means so much to you and you don't want anything to jeopardize that.

"Oh, Michael, stop this. Please. I'm tired. I don't want to play this game. Don't go tomorrow if you don't want to, for whatever reason. Go show a house. Or not. Go play racquet-ball. Sit here and brood. Do whatever you want to do but don't make it my issue. I'm going to pick up my mom in the morning and go to Sophie and Pete's."

He clenched his jaw but said nothing. He looked at his feet, at the bed and then back up at my face. He took a deep breath and then he turned and walked away.

Thirty

—◦❧◦—

The house was buzzing when my mother and I arrived. All the out-of-town guests were there, about twenty of them, along with immediate family. Sophie waved from the kitchen and carried a casserole dish to the dining room table, which was laden with food and flowers and coffee urns and wine bottles. Pete walked around pouring champagne. Soft jazz played; people talked and laughed. It was a festival of activity.

Patrick was bringing pitchers of orange juice to the table when he saw me. His face shone and that made me very happy I'd come. He wore the turtleneck we'd bought together when he came to Chicago for lunch. It was soft heather-gray cashmere and looked gorgeous with charcoal gray pants, and the black loafers that shone within an inch of their lives. He shined them for me, I thought, and grinned at him. He grinned back. "No Michael?" he asked.

"He had a showing."

Patrick hid his disappointment well.

"That boy works too hard," my mother said, although on the way over I'd told her the reason for his brunch boycott.

"Hmmmph . . ." was all she'd said.

"So nice to see you this morning," Patrick said, and kissed my cheek and then my mother's. "You both look beautiful."

"So do you," I said. "Nice sweater."

"Thanks. I can't take all the credit. I had help picking it out."

"Come on, everybody," Sophie called. "Plates are on the buffet. Fill them and find a seat wherever. Holler if you need anything."

Patrick ushered my mother to a seat on the sofa and said he'd make her a plate if she saved us seats. She said she would if he made her a mimosa.

"She's great," Patrick said as we walked away. "I'm sorry I didn't get to meet your dad."

Patrick's closeness sent electric currents up my spine as we walked to the dining room.

"Where'd you stay last night?" I asked.

"Here," he said. "On the foldout couch in the den. We were up till three this morning." He laughed. "I haven't done that since high school." I thought of New Year's Eve thirty years ago. "It was fun. Danielle and Chris were here until two-thirty and then had to boogie to grab their bags for a flight at six to Honolulu. They're really fun. It's been a kick getting to know Pete and Sophie's girls."

Sophie had made caramel-apple French toast for the brunch, and several casseroles were filled with her famous egg strata. There was crisp bacon, sausage, fruit salad and mimosas. Iris centerpieces from the wedding were scattered around the dining room.

"Jesus," I said, "when did she have time to do all this?"

"Last night. She was like Rachael Ray on steroids, ordering us around like we were her sous-chefs."

I was jealous that I hadn't been part of the fun.

As we ate, my mother grilled Patrick about his life in Florida: what did he do, where did he live, how many kids did he have, did he exercise, did he cook, did he read the newspaper. I tried giving her a look to get her to let up but she ignored me. Patrick answered easily, not seeming to mind, or even to notice, really. He threw questions back at her when she left a millisecond of silence. "What's your favorite movie?" "How'd you meet your husband?"

When he and I reached for the syrup at the same time, fingers touching, nearly spilling it, I felt my mother's eyes on me, on us. She paused for a moment and then she said to him, "Did you ever think about getting married again?"

I slugged down the rest of my mimosa.

Tiffany wandered through the house snapping pictures, posing everyone in little groups. She tried to take a picture of my mother, Patrick and me but my mother said, "Oh, just take one of the two of them. I don't like pictures of myself at my age," and she got up and moved off. Patrick put his arm over my shoulder and we leaned our heads close. "Oh, that's cute," Tiffany said, looking at the display, then showing it to me. It was.

Tiffany's hair was spiked today and her piercings were in their full glory, filled with shiny hoops and studs. Later she cornered me in the kitchen to tell me that Ryan had asked her to go steady.

"Oh, cool," I said. "Did he give you a ring?" I remembered wearing Patrick's class ring on a chain around my neck.

"A ring? No. But he changed his Facebook page to 'In a relationship,'" she said, grinning. "He asked me to go to his prom."

"Fun. You can wear your bridesmaid dress," I said.

She made a face. "Or not," she said. "I'm done with that

thing." Then her face softened and she touched my arm. "No offense."

"None taken."

"I *love* Patrick," Tiffany said. "We all had so much fun last night."

"I heard. He likes you, too."

"He likes you, too," she said.

"Why do you say that?"

"He talked about you all night. Asked all kinds of questions about you."

"He did not," I said, pleased.

"Did, too," Sophie said, coming up behind me with a stack of dirty dishes and giving me a bump with her hip. She raised her eyebrows, Groucho Marx style. Tiffany snapped our picture as we laughed.

"Help me with the desserts, would you, Lib?" Sophie said, bringing out large, flat pastry boxes. I unwrapped the goodies—tiny zucchini muffins, chocolate squares with satiny frosting, cookies—and put them on plates, and Tiffany snapped another picture as I stuffed a muffin into my mouth. Then she went off in search of other photographic subjects, or maybe her "steady."

Sophie said, "He *was* asking a lot of questions."

"About what?"

"Oh, just about what you'd been up to all these years. What you liked to do. If you were going to marry Michael."

"What'd you say to that one?"

"I told him to ask you." She got small plates from the cupboard and the "Danielle and Christopher"–embossed napkins. "Are you?" she asked.

"That's the sixty-four-thousand-dollar question," I said. "Hey, did something happen last night when the guys were smoking their cigars?"

"Pete said there was a little tension but it wasn't a big deal. Michael apparently made it clear he wasn't about to bond with Patrick."

"I suppose that's to be expected," I said.

"Kind of childish," she said.

"He's jealous. How would you feel if you were in his place?"

"Depends on if I had anything to worry about." She piled silverware on a big black-lacquered tray. "Does he?"

"I guess he thinks he does."

Sophie leaned on the granite countertop and looked me in the eye. "But does he?"

Sometimes when I look at Sophie's face my heart swells with the familiarity of every angle, every line, how dear it is to me, how it holds all of our history. "I don't know, Soph," I said. "I really don't know."

Thirty-one

—◦ ❧ ◦—

All the guests had gone. My mother hitched a ride home with Sophie's parents, which left Sophie, Pete, Tiffany, Patrick and me on clean-up duty. Pete put on some seventies music and we danced around the kitchen, tossing towels to each other, wrapping food, washing dishes, singing to the music.

When "Cat's in the Cradle" came on, the four adults sang along.

Tiffany hooted when we got to the "little boy blue, man in the moon" part. "What the heck is this?" she asked.

"Harry Chapin!" we said in unison.

"Remember when we went to Purdue to see him in concert?" Patrick said.

"Yeah," I said. "I told my parents I was staying at Sophie's that night."

"And I told my parents I was staying at your house," Sophie said.

"And we stayed in Purdue at that guest house where that lady had four dogs and a big, honking mole on her eyelid."

Our laughter bounced off the oak cabinets, wrapping us all in memories.

"The four of you stayed at a guest house?" the forgotten Tiffany asked, sitting on the counter watching us as if we were a double feature.

Oops.

"Patrick and me in one room, the girls in another," Pete lied. "And don't you try that staying-at-your-girlfriend's story on us. Don't think we won't be checking. We know all the tricks, sweet pea."

Tiffany was smart enough not to answer.

"You sound just like your father," Sophie told him, and he swatted her on the butt.

"Didn't Denny Cavanaugh and Jess Silver meet us there?" Patrick said. "Remember them?"

"Yeah. I still play poker with Denny," Pete said.

"No kidding," Patrick said. "What's he up to these days? Wait. Let me guess. He's an auto mechanic."

"Nope."

"A roofer?"

"Nope."

"A drug dealer?"

Pete laughed. "No, he's an English teacher."

Patrick could barely contain his laughter. "Cavanaugh, an English teacher? That's a good one." He ran his fingers through his hair. "He was such a burnout. What about Jess? Do you know what happened to her?"

"They got married after college and had three kids," Sophie said. "Got divorced about eight years later, married other people, had a few more kids. Then they both got divorced again and about ten years ago they married each other again and had another kid."

"So between the two of them," Pete said, "they have eight kids. The oldest is close to thirty and the youngest is nine."

"Whew! More power to them with all those kids. But that's cool that they got back together again after all those years. Very cool." Patrick shook his head. "I sure wouldn't want to raise kids today."

"Why not?" Tiffany asked.

"Too old," Patrick said. "Grandkids are just the thing at my age. You get to be the fun one, you get to choose how much time to spend with them, then send them off when you're tired and let their parents discipline them. It's perfect." He tossed a pot to me to hang on the rack near my head. And when "Stayin' Alive" came on the stereo he beat out the rhythm with a wooden spoon on Tiffany's knee. Then he grabbed my hand and we did a little disco move. Pete and Sophie joined in and Tiffany couldn't stop laughing.

"You guys are too much," she said.

"She means 'too old,' " Patrick said, winking, and twirled me. Then we went into the across-the-shoulder move we'd done so long ago. Tiffany thrust two fingers in her mouth, let out a shrill whistle and said, "The German judge gives you a nine-point-nine."

I was breathless and wound up, caught up in the nostalgia of it and the four of us being together again, basking in Tiffany's admiration. In some ways it felt like old times but in others it felt bright and shiny and new. Patrick's hand on my arm gave off sparks that seemed to flutter around and settle on my skin. His face wasn't as familiar as it used to be but his touch was, and his laugh, and the easy way he held me.

When the song came to an end he pulled me close and

wrapped his arms around me. "We've still got it," he said. We all clapped and laughed and high-fived each other and Tiffany shouted, "The German judge just changed his score to a perfect ten!"

Thirty-two

~··~

Patrick had found a moment in between dancing and cleaning to ask if I would drive him to the airport. And I had found a moment to say yes, even as I wondered if Michael was at my house, waiting for my return.

"This has been a gas," Patrick said on our way to O'Hare. "Sophie and Pete are just like they always were. I mean, none of us looks the same but we're the same people inside, aren't we?"

"I'm glad you came," I said. "Sophie and Pete are, too."

"So, you gonna come visit me in Florida?"

I looked over at him and smiled. "That'd be nice, wouldn't it?"

"Then do it, Lib."

"I wish it were that easy."

"I know it's not easy. I know things are complicated for you," he said, and put his hand on my shoulder. "But sometimes we make things more complicated than they need to be. Sometimes the solutions are right in front of us."

"What do you mean?"

"Marry me, Lib," he said, and I almost sideswiped a red Toyota. "Don't marry Michael. Marry me."

I could feel his eyes on me. My heart felt as if it would thump through my rib cage. *"Marry* you? Oh my god." No one had mentioned the word "marriage" to me in a hundred years (except my parents, of course) and now it was all anyone could talk about.

He laughed. "Okay, don't freak. You don't have to marry me. Just come live with me."

"Oh, Patrick. What are you saying? We don't even know each other anymore."

He took his hand away, leaving my shoulder cold and empty. "We haven't changed," he said. "We know each other like we knew each other thirty years ago. We have the same connection now that we had then." He turned his body toward me, a serious look on his face. "It's like Denny Cavanaugh and Jess. They had a connection that couldn't be broken even though they left each other for a while. Sometimes that happens."

I couldn't deny what he was saying. I couldn't say it hadn't occurred to me. But there was the other side to that coin as well; the side that said what we'd had was a high school love affair, that's all, not the real world.

"I'm not going to deny there's still a connection," I said. "But all the living we've done has changed us. We've had these experiences and relationships, and all that can't help but change us from what we were back then into who we are now. Yes, maybe basically we're the same people, but so much life has to have affected us in ways we can't even calculate."

We approached the departures terminal. Soon he would be on a plane and I might never see him again. I pulled over to the curb. People bustled around us, getting luggage out of trunks, hugging goodbye.

"Look, Lib," Patrick said, his brown eyes intense. "I love you." He *loved* me? How could he say that? He put up his hand when I started to interrupt. "That's not up for debate. Whether you believe it or not, it's true. It's clear to me. We've wasted enough time. We're not getting any younger. We've missed out on thirty-some years but we don't have to miss out on the next thirty." I thought my head was going to explode. "So just come and visit me," he said. "Take some time, get away for a little while. Forget the marriage part; I didn't mean that."

"You didn't mean it?" I said.

"Well, not for now anyway. Not so long ago I was giving you a lecture about making too many life changes, wasn't I? So we'll take our time. You need some time to heal from the loss of your dad and we don't need to rush into anything. You need to be sure that whatever you do, you do for the right reasons. But let's spend a little time together—a few days, a week—and see what happens."

"I'm just not sure this is a good time," I said. Why wasn't I saying, *Great! I'm on my way?*

"It's the best time," Patrick said and took my hand. "You owe it to yourself." When he saw the look on my face he said, "No, really, you do. And you owe it to Michael, and believe me I'm not his cheerleader. But if there's even the smallest part of you that's considering it, you need to find out, even if it means discovering I'm wrong. At least you won't end up married to Michael and wondering what might have happened."

Part of me wanted to go with him now, right this minute. Really . . . did I want to live the rest of my life with a "what-if" hovering over me?

He cupped my chin, kissed me sweetly, swept the hair off my forehead. "Think about it, okay?"

His face was so close, his breath a whisper on my face. I felt dizzy. "I will," I said.

He smiled broadly. "Okay, great. That's good enough for me."

✣

I could think of nothing else as I lay in bed that night. I imagined Patrick picking me up at the airport in . . . what? I didn't even know what kind of car he drove. An SUV? Volkswagen? Mercedes? Rusted-out Impala? So we'd drive in this mystery car through the streets of his town lined with palm trees and pink stucco houses, and pull up in front of his place—which would be what? A house, a condo, a beach shack? I didn't even know. Maybe it was a mansion. Maybe a double-wide trailer. Maybe he was one of those hoarders you see on television and every surface was buried under piles of crap.

I knew nothing about this man.

Would we stand there awkwardly, not knowing what to do or say? And where would I sleep?

Questions rocketed through my brain, shoving sleep right out the door. I lay on my back examining the landscape of the ceiling. Rufus jumped up and looked into my eyes, meowed in his squeaky, mournful way and then climbed onto my chest and lay there purring. I closed my eyes and tried counting sheep. I got to eighty-five of those fluffy little critters jumping over an imagined white picket fence, but my mind was on speed dial, recalling Patrick saying I should marry him, the softness in his eyes when he looked at me, Michael's bruised expression when I'd told him I was going to the brunch without him. So I sent little Michaels over that fence and counted them instead, and then little Patricks. They were good jumpers.

I would go. I knew that. Even though I also knew it was going to be a huge problem for Michael, an obstacle he might not be able to get past. But Patrick was right—if I didn't, I'd always wonder. Chances were so slim that this could work, but I had to find out.

It was past midnight when I picked up the phone to call him, past one A.M. his time, but I didn't hesitate.

"I'm coming to visit," I said when he sleepily answered the phone. There was silence and I started to think he'd changed his mind but then he said, "Mom?"

I laughed and laughed.

"I'm so glad," he said in a wide-awake and delighted voice. And then, "Whoa, I better look for my vacuum cleaner."

The pleasure in his voice jumped right through the wires and landed happily in my heart.

When I finally slept I had a dream that Michael and Patrick were in a track-and-field event and were neck and neck as they jumped over hurdles toward the finish line.

I didn't need Freud to interpret that one.

Thirty-three

B right and early the next day I got online and looked for tickets to Florida. I found a good fare and convenient times, and selected a return for four days later. When I got to the screen with the button that said, *Book this reservation*, I had a moment's doubt. Michael was going to freak. One thing was sure, he wasn't going to say, "Oh yeah, I understand, go ahead, spend all the time you want with Patrick. Sleep with him if you need to. I'll be here waiting when you get back."

I wavered for a second. And then clicked the button. *Your reservation is confirmed*, the screen told me and I laughed out loud. Immediately I sent off an e-mail to Patrick with the details of my flight. *I'm nervous*, I wrote, *but looking forward to spending time with you.*

Now I had to tell Michael. I picked up the phone and dialed, but hung up before I punched in the last number. This was terrible timing. He was probably on his way to work and it seemed mean to tell him while he was driving, right before he went into the office. Or worse, saw a client. This wasn't the kind of news anyone wants to start the day with. I'd call him tonight when he was home, alone. Where there was scotch in his liquor cabinet.

I went for a run instead.

When I got back the red light on my answering machine was blinking.

"Great, Libby." Patrick's mellow tones filled my living room. "Can't wait to see you. And there's nothing to be nervous about. I'll be at the airport, in the terminal outside the gate area, with a big sign that says CARSON PARTY. We'll go right down to the beach and have lunch at an outdoor café and drink something with an umbrella in it and eat soft-shell crabs. How does that sound?" I could hear the smile popping off his face. "Bring warm-weather clothes. The temps are still in the eighties. See you in a few days."

Oh god. What have I done? I thought.

I called Sophie.

"Well, *good*," she said when I told her what I was doing.

"Really?"

"Yes, really. It's time you did what you wanted to do instead of what everyone else wants."

"Who is this?" I said. "Aren't you the one who told me Michael would be a great husband? That he'd be someone to spend the rest of my life with?"

"Oh, fuck that," Sophie said. "I've seen you and Patrick together. Go see what happens. Michael's not going anywhere."

"He'll be furious. He won't put up with this."

"Yes, he'll say that. He'll tell you you're through, but that's the thing about Michael. He's steady and he's forgiving and he loves you. He'll get over it if you find out Patrick's not the one."

"It seems so cruel to do this to him."

"Well, it's not the nicest thing in the world. But would it

be better to marry him and then find out you were in love with someone else?"

"How do I tell him?"

"You say, 'So, Michael, I'm going to go see Patrick in Florida for a couple days and you're not invited.' And then you hang up."

ꝣ

While I was still riding high from Sophie's encouragement I called Michael. Voice mail.

"Michael, it's me. I know you're pissed that I went to the brunch yesterday. I hope you're feeling better today and that you'll still be here on Wednesday as usual. I'm counting on it, okay? I'll make dinner and we'll talk. Call me."

I didn't hear from him that day.

I had work I needed to complete and deliver before I left: to finish the details on a blazer I was making for one client, hem three pairs of pants for another, alter a suit for a third, and work on Bea Rosatti's wedding ensemble. So I put some CDs in the stereo and Maroon 5 serenaded me as I stitched in the lining on the black wool blazer. If I moved fast, I could deliver it tomorrow and still have a couple of days to finish the rest. As I worked I tried not to feel too bad about Michael or too good about Patrick. I didn't know what I'd do if Michael didn't come over Wednesday or call me before Friday, when I was leaving. Part of me thought, Good, I'll just go and not tell him and decide what to do when I get back. The coward's way out always seems easiest, doesn't it?

Thirty-four

—∂ ᴥ ∂—

Tuesday came and went and still no word from Michael. It seemed I was in a familiar pattern with him, alternating between pissed off and guilty. One minute I'd pick up the phone to call him and the next minute I'd slam down the phone and say, "Fuck you. Two can play at this game."

On Wednesday, though, I went to the grocery store and picked up a whole chicken, some potatoes and fixings for salad. My game plan was to assume he was coming over, that he'd have called if that weren't the case. If I was wrong, I was wrong. I sort of hoped I was.

In the afternoon the kitchen smelled homey with the chicken roasting in the oven, stuffed with onions, lemons, thyme, oregano and parsley. I was peeling potatoes when I heard Michael's key in the door. My stomach did a spin.

"Smells good," he said, coming into the kitchen, coat still on. He didn't kiss me as he usually did. He barely looked at me. Instead he got a glass and poured some scotch.

"I wasn't sure you were coming," I said. I cut the potatoes

into wedges and put them on a baking pan. "It would have been nice if you'd called me back."

"Yeah, I know. But I wasn't sure what I was doing until I got here." He took a slug of scotch while I drizzled the potatoes with olive oil and sprinkled them with salt, pepper and rosemary. "I've been thinking a lot about what's going on with you," he said, leaning against the refrigerator, "and I think it must be related to your dad's death." The word brought tears to my eyes but I blinked them away and put the potatoes in the oven.

He went on. "Grief affects people in different ways. It's a big blow and I understand that. I think it's hard to be yourself right now and I'm sorry you're going through it."

His empathy softened me. "It is a tough time," I admitted.

"I think you need time to work through that before you can worry about anything else." He seemed relieved to have figured it all out. "I'll be honest, it's not easy to deal with, but I'll try to be patient. Losing someone close to us can make us say and do things we wouldn't ordinarily do. I understand that now. And I forgive you."

My head snapped up. *"Forgive* me?"

"Oh, I don't mean *forgive* exactly. That was a bad choice of words. I just mean I can overlook what's going on with you now because you're grieving."

I guess I should have appreciated his empathy, but I hated how sure he was of himself, how pleased that he'd decoded me. I hated the smug expression on his face.

"What'd you do, Google 'grief'?" I said.

"Well, I did actually. It's amazing what you can learn on the Internet."

Can you learn not to be an asshole? I wondered.

"I'm going to Florida on Friday," I said quietly. *Can you forgive that?*

Michael blinked. He looked into his glass and then back at me, studying every detail of my face as if he weren't sure who he was looking at.

"Well, that's an interesting way to deal with your grief," he said. I had to look away. "Goddamn it, Libby," he said. "I never thought you'd do this to me."

My chest tightened. "I didn't do anything to you," I said. *Yet.* "There's nothing going on that you don't know about."

"Yeah, right," he said. "That's why you're going to Florida."

It sounded bad. I knew it did. "Nothing's going on," I said again. "I don't even know how I feel about him."

"You don't know how you feel about him. You don't know how you feel about me," he said, his eyes on fire. "Just exactly what *do* you know?"

Where had Mr. Understanding gone?

"I guess I don't know much of anything anymore."

Michael walked over to the window and stared out. He twisted the wand on the miniblinds, opening, closing, straightening them. "You think he's so great, Libby? You don't even know him." He turned. "You have no idea who he is. But you're going to throw this all away." He waved his hands, sweeping the room.

I looked around the room. "Throw all *what* away?" I said. "This is *my* house. My TV, my Oriental rug, my candlesticks, my pictures hanging on the walls—"

"You know what I mean," he said. "Us. Our future. Our life." He stood for a moment, glaring at me, his shoulders hunched, his mouth grim. Then he huffed and turned away. He poured more scotch, adding water this time, and left the kitchen.

I braced myself against the counter, my heart beating

like a jackhammer. The smell of the chicken was intense, so I opened the oven to see if it was done. I took the bird out and studied the golden, perfectly crisped skin. I breathed deeply for several moments and then went into the living room, where Michael was sitting on the ottoman, his head in his hands. Was he *crying*? He sat utterly still and there was no sound. I wished I could make him disappear so I wouldn't have to see the dejected curve of his back, his vulnerable neck, white where the barber had trimmed his hair. I wished I could spare him this, and spare myself this overwhelming feeling of being a traitor. And a bitch.

Rufus was curled into a gray ball on the chair. I moved him and sat in front of Michael.

He looked up. Thankfully his eyes were dry.

"I can't believe this." He laughed but there was no amusement in it. "Two weeks ago I was the happiest guy on earth. What the hell happened? Does what we have mean nothing to you?"

"What do we have, Michael? What we *had* meant a lot to me, back when we first met, when we had the same goals, when we seemed to be on the same page about our life together. I never wanted to get married again, you knew that. You said you felt the same way.

"Two weeks ago you may have been the happiest guy on earth, but at what cost? If making yourself happy makes me miserable, what have we got?"

His shoulders slumped, face etched with misery. "Don't go, Libby."

I felt overwhelmingly sad, for him, for me, for the circumstances, for the fact that my dad was dead. What would my father say if he could see all this?

"Michael . . ." I didn't know what to say.

"You know how long I was single before I met you? Fifteen

years. And I was fine. I figured I'd had my chance and it didn't work out. You know how hard it is to meet someone at our age?" I nodded. "And then I met you." I swallowed. "And you changed my life." Don't tell me any more, I thought. "I mean, it's not like I didn't have a great life—I did. I had friends, I had a good business, I traveled. And all that was terrific. But you know what? It was a hundred times more terrific with you in it."

I went to sit beside him and he moved over to accommodate me. I couldn't speak for a moment. I took his hand. "I know what you're saying. I've felt some of that myself. It is nicer to have someone to share things with. And it's even better if you have a great life to begin with. I think you appreciate it even more then." He nodded and I started crying then. "I wouldn't hurt you for anything in the world," I said. "And I don't want to lose you and everything we've built together. But you're right, I'm not myself right now. I'm doubting everything—you, me, my own feelings, my goals, what I want out of life. The bottom line is, I can't tell you I won't go see Patrick. Don't you see that I have to be sure? No matter how I feel about you, I need to be sure. I'm too old to have regrets.

"You're so important to me," I said. "But would you want to get married if I'm not sure? What chance would we have?"

He said nothing. He put his elbows on his knees, head down. I reached out but my hand just hovered over his shoulder, and I withdrew it.

He stood up then, and rolled his head on his neck. "I think we'd be fine," he said, straightening. "I think once you made the decision you'd realize how right it is."

"I wish I could be sure of that."

"I know." He shook his head, picked up his glass and took it into the kitchen, leaving me and Rufus sitting there. In a minute he came back and said, "I'm gonna go."

"Don't leave yet," I said. I thought if we talked it through I'd unearth something important. Maybe together we'd figure something out. I didn't want him to leave with all this emptiness, and my guilt, hanging between us.

"Why not? What else is there to say?" he said. "You made your decision to go see Patrick. What that says is pretty clear to me, Libby. I don't need an instruction manual to see I'm not on your agenda."

My throat felt tight. Why was I doing this to him? "I'm sorry, Michael, I really am."

He didn't look as if he believed me but he said, "I know." And then, "But really, so what?" I flinched. He sighed, smiled thinly and walked to the front door, head high, shoulders square.

"Are you okay?" I asked.

"Oh yeah, I'm just peachy." He turned. "Have fun, Libby. Have a great time with your boyfriend. But don't expect me to be waiting when it doesn't work out."

I watched him walk out and close the door behind him. I stood there waiting for him to come back in. And as I stood Rufus wound himself around my legs.

But Michael didn't come back, and I realized I had just doused that bridge in gasoline and ignited it.

A painful thing settled inside me while tears coursed down my face.

Thirty-five

Thursday morning I went for a long run, hoping the exercise would exhaust my brain enough that it would stop functioning for a while. I didn't want to make any more decisions. I didn't want to overthink what I was doing. Should I go? Shouldn't I? Should I call Patrick and tell him I wasn't coming? Should I call Michael and suggest we just go to city hall and get married?

When I ran past my favorite house, *Michael's house,* I felt sick to my stomach. It could be the perfect home. Michael had no problem spending the money to make it whatever I wanted. Hadn't I always wanted to live there? Hadn't I always said that you'd just have to be happy if you lived in a house like that? Ultimately, though, I knew that that wasn't true. It was just a house. It had no power to make anyone happy.

Jill and I went to Mom's later in the day. She had asked us to help her clean out the closet and sort Dad's things. "See if Sophie can come, too," she'd said. "Dad thought of her like another daughter." So the four of us stared at his side of the closet, at all those suits lined up like soldiers: white shirts, then blue, shiny wingtips underneath.

"Let's do the dresser first," my mother said. We opened the drawers and pulled out sweaters, T-shirts, socks. I held his sweaters up to my face and breathed in his smell. How could we give these away when he was still alive in them? "I'm going to take a couple of these," I said. "Maybe Michael will wear them." I wasn't kidding anyone—Michael was much larger than my father—but no one felt compelled to point that out. Sophie stacked handkerchiefs and pajamas on the bed and Jill sorted them into boxes while my mother and I went through his workout clothes: velour sweat pants with matching jackets in varying jewel tones—emerald, garnet.

"Remember when he rode his bike up to the Botanic Garden?" Mom said. It was at least forty miles from here and he'd set out in the morning with a bottle of water and three granola bars. "It started raining in the afternoon and it was dark before he got back. I was so worried, I was about to call the police when he finally walked in the door looking like something the cat dragged in."

"He was in bed for a week after that with a bad cold," Jill said. "He got lost on the way back, but god forbid he should ask someone for directions."

"He was a stubborn one," Mom said with a heartbreaking little smile.

Inside I felt as empty as those drawers by the time we moved on to his jewelry box.

"I want you all to take some things," Mom said. There were about twenty sets of cuff links, rings and pocket watches, penknives and money clips, tie tacks, coins, some of which I remembered buying for him when Jill and I were little. There was a bracelet made with tiny beads of turquoise and silver that I'd made for Father's Day when I was in Girl Scouts. He never wore it, except the day I gave it to him—he never wore bracelets—but he'd kept it all these years. I put it in my pile.

There was a small silver frame on his dresser with a picture of Dad with Jill and me when we were about three and five. He was kneeling on the grass with an arm around each of us and we were in matching plaid dresses, our hair in pigtails. I put that in my pile, too.

Mom had put out the tea set we'd always loved, the white porcelain one with pink cabbage roses on it, and dainty cups with fragile handles. We sat in the living room in front of the fireplace and drank tea spiked with brandy and told Dad stories: the time he chased the neighbor's dog through the yard in his boxers because the mutt had stolen the newspaper. Or the time he decided to be a good guy and do the family laundry and accidentally washed Mom's favorite watch, the one he'd given her for a wedding present.

"Can you girls come back tomorrow and help me with his office?" Mom asked.

"Sure," Sophie and Jill said. My mother looked at me.

Uh-oh. "Um, I can't," I said. Because I'll be in Florida cheating on my fiancé.

"Why not?" Jill asked. Sophie sipped her tea.

"I'm going away for the weekend."

"Oh, where are you going?"

To hell, probably. "Florida," I said boldly, as if there were nothing wrong with this picture.

"What's in Florida?" my mother asked.

Jill's eyes grew wide. "Patrick!" She said it as if she'd discovered gold. "You're going to spend the weekend with Patrick?" I nodded. "Is Michael going with you?"

Sophie let out a little choked laugh and we all looked at her. "Sorry," she said.

My mother drank her tea, knobby fingers grasping the cup, pinky in the air. "What does Michael think about that?" she asked.

"I'm sure he's thrilled," Jill said. "Did you leave the tags on that wedding dress?"

I fingered the sweater in my lap, my dad's sweater, the light blue cashmere one.

"Patrick told me he loves me." The silence was thick around me. Everyone stared. Mother put down her cup. "I know," I said. "It seems pretty silly, doesn't it, after all these years?"

"Wow." Sophie.

"Jesus." Jill.

"Oh, Libby." Mom.

Her disapproving tone caught me off guard and made me feel fifteen. How old do you have to be before you feel like a grown-up with your parents?

"How do you feel about him?" Sophie asked.

"I don't know. Attracted. Confused. Overwhelmed. Guilty. Excited."

"Don't get caught up in this, Libby," my mother said. "He's a very appealing man and I can see how you'd be attracted to him, but he's not in love with you." How did she know? Maybe he was. It was *possible*, wasn't it? "It's absurd," she said. "You haven't seen each other since high school."

I bristled. "Jeez, Mom, one minute you're telling me you think Michael's *right enough*." I said the words with disdain. "Not Mr. Right but right enough. And now when I think you might be right and that I should check this out, you say it's absurd." Jill tried to head me off with a placating look but I paid no attention. "Who knows? Yeah, it's unlikely, but it's not absurd. Strange things happen in life."

"I just don't want you to throw away everything you have

with Michael for a man you hardly know." She leaned forward. "Think about what you're doing."

"Mom," Jill said, but I interrupted her.

"You know what, Mom? I don't need you to tell me how stupid I'm being."

"Libby. I'm not saying you're being stupid."

"I already feel terrible for Michael and I'm sorry I hurt him. I feel terrible that we've gone so far with the wedding plans and that I bought that dress and that he bought that damn house." I couldn't stop my voice from getting louder. "I should have listened to my instinct in the very beginning and given us both time to think about it. But I didn't and things got out of control and I didn't know how to stop it. And then Patrick comes into my life and fucks everything up." I stopped. I'd never said anything more than "shit" in front of my mother. "Sorry." She waved it away. "But the fact is, I have feelings for him."

She looked small and troubled. "Excuse me," she said and left the room. So now I could add her to the list of people I'd injured. This woman who'd just spent the last few hours sorting through the belongings of her dead husband, the man she'd lived with and adored for more than fifty years. What was wrong with me? Why couldn't I just nod and tell her yes, I'd think about what I was doing?

Sophie came over. She put her arm around me and spoke quietly. "Relax, Lib. Your mom's just trying to help."

"You mean talk some sense into me, don't you?"

"No. She's just worried."

Jill said, "She wants you to be happy. She doesn't care who it's with. She already told you that. She's just afraid that you'll figure out that Michael's who you should be with and by that time he'll be gone."

"I'm afraid of that, too," I said. "But what should I do?

Marry him and regret it later? That'd be fun, to have three divorces under my belt. You know what? You guys are all making me crazy. You're so wishy-washy—yes Michael, no Michael, yes Patrick, no Patrick. *What? Make up your minds!*"

Why couldn't they just tell me what to do once and for all, step by step, complete with a diagram: how to handle everyone, what to say, when to say it, what to do and how to live with the consequences.

Shouldn't life be simple by the time you're fifty?

"It's not our minds that need to be made up," Jill said. "It's yours. Just explain to Mom how you're feeling. She'll understand."

"No, she won't. My whole life she's judged me. She never thought I knew what I was doing. She always thought I should do things differently. I should have stayed married, I should have stayed in my job—"

"No, I didn't," my mother said. I turned to see her standing in the kitchen doorway. "I always thought you were very brave in your decisions because your decisions always scared me." She sat down across from me. "Your father and I just wanted you to be safe. I guess we wanted you to be more like us, more conventional. It frightened us to see you taking so many chances, from the time you were a little girl. You rode your tricycle blocks and blocks before we could catch you, you went out for the hockey team when you could have been a cheerleader, you went to college a thousand miles away, you quit a good-paying job to start your own business. It all scared the hell out of us," she said. "We wanted you to be safe and secure. We wanted you to be content. But you never were. You were always moving on to the next thing."

"Is that so terrible?" I said, tears pooling in my eyes.

"No, sweetheart." She took my hands. "We were always in awe of you. You've lived your life the way you wanted to and you've been successful. You've made some risky deci-sions but they've mostly paid off and we couldn't have been prouder. Your father was so admiring of your guts." Now tears were dropping onto my dad's sweater, *plop, plop, plop.* "Do what you feel is right, Libby. Go to Patrick, if that's what you feel."

"I feel like if I don't check it out I'll be sorry for the rest of my life," I said, my voice cracking.

"Then go. If that's how you feel then you need to go. You need to be happy. And whatever makes you happy is my happiness, too." She took a napkin off the table and wiped my fifty-year-old face. "I'm not saying I won't worry, though."

I hugged her, hard. The bones in her back felt sturdy and I let that energy seep into my core. The coziness of the living room consoled me, this room I'd spent my life in, each chair and pillow and doily utterly cozy and familiar. I grew up in-dependent and powerful in this house, confident and strong. I grew up making my own decisions and dealing with the consequences no matter how they turned out.

As if she were tuned in to my thoughts, my mother said, "However it turns out, everything will work out for the best. You've always been good at figuring things out and working through obstacles that come your way. You're unflappable, Libby. You need to follow your own heart, not someone else's. Including Daddy's. Go. See what happens."

Thirty-six

—◌ ❦ ◌—

Friday. Finally. I hadn't slept much so I was up early folding a pair of jeans, two pairs of shorts, some capri pants and two shirts and placing them in my suitcase. The weather was in the eighties, Patrick had said. I had no idea what we would be doing. Kayaking? Hiking? Lying on the beach? I threw in a bathing suit and a long skirt that could be casual or dressy with the right top and accessories. The air in the bedroom shimmered around me and I felt lighter than I had in weeks, maybe months. I packed a pair of tan sandals, some black strappy shoes, my running shoes. What else did I need? Something to sleep in. But what? I folded an oversized T-shirt and laid it carefully in my suitcase, and at the last minute I added a sexy, short nightgown. Just in case.

Traffic on the Kennedy Expressway was heavy and as the taxi inched along I imagined my reunion with Patrick. In my mind I could see him standing there waiting, a big smile lighting up his handsome face. I could see us hugging while people moved all around us smiling approvingly. I couldn't picture what would happen next or where this would lead, but there was a balloon of anticipation all around me.

The terminal was crowded as I walked to my gate: businesspeople off to work, vacationers in T-shirts and sandals, families happily heading toward their adventures. I walked briskly, smiling at little children passing by, admiring the glazed doughnuts in the cases along the concourse. Bright sunlight shone in through the windows, freshening the tile walls. At the gate the ticket agent told me, "Sorry, but I only have center seats left. In the back."

I smiled brightly. "That's great, perfect, thank you so much," I said, as if I'd just scored a front-row seat for a Paul McCartney concert.

As we flew over North Carolina I thought about Patrick when we were young, clearly remembering the details of his eighteen-year-old body—his jutting hip bones, smooth muscular back, firm butt. I thought about how his narrow, hairless chest felt against mine, and the size and hardness of his penis, the first I'd ever seen. I couldn't help comparing it to Michael's, thinking it was a little smaller but appreciably harder. But how fair is it to compare the erection of an eighteen-year-old to that of a sixty-year-old, especially when thirty years had passed to distort the image?

There was a sob from the woman beside me and I turned to look at her. She was looking out the window, wiping her eyes and shoveling food into her mouth from an assortment of snack-sized bags.

"Are you all right?" I asked. She stopped chewing and shoveling, and was completely still as if waiting for me to vanish. When I didn't she turned to look at me.

"Are you talking to me?" she asked in a small voice. She had messy dark hair that framed her small face. Her skin was elegant and unlined. Baby skin. She'd cried all of her makeup off except for small smudges of black under her eyes.

"Yes, I'm sorry. I don't mean to intrude, but are you okay? Can I do anything for you?"

"I'm fine," she said and attempted a smile. It failed, and tears trailed down her cheeks. "I'm sorry," she said, waving her hand in front of her face as if that would make the tears disappear. She had a southern accent and a musical voice. Her fingernails were chewed up and her red nail polish chipped off.

"Want some?" She offered me one of the bags. The one with the Gummi bears.

"No, thanks."

"Triscuits?" she said, offering another bag. I smiled and shook my head.

"I always eat when I'm upset," she said. "I can't help it. It's the only thing that helps."

"It doesn't seem to be working."

She laughed briefly but just as quickly the laugh was gone. "Ice cream is really the best, but it's kind of hard to bring on an airplane."

"I'm sorry you're upset. Do you want to talk?" I asked.

Her face crumpled again and she put down the bags to pull a tissue out of her purse and wipe at her eyes.

"My boyfriend and I broke up," she said.

"I'm so sorry."

"Yeah, well, it was my idea."

"Then why are you crying?" I asked.

"I don't know," she said, her voice rising. Her eyes welled up and she reached into one of the bags and shoveled Gummis into her mouth. "I don't know if it was the right thing to do," she said with her mouth full. "I feel so awful. If it was the right thing, why would I feel so awful?"

"Change is hard," I said. "Why did you break up with him?"

"He's boring." We looked at each other. And then I laughed, a big "Hah!" escaping from my throat before I could stop it.

"I know," she said. "That's terrible, isn't it?"

"No, it's not," I said. "I was just expecting something more concrete, like he cheated on you or he beat you or something."

"I wish he had. Well, not beat me, but something that would give me a good reason." She chewed heartily and wiped at her eyes.

"How long were you together?"

"We've known each other practically our whole lives." She pronounced it *lavs.* "We started dating in high school, six years ago. I never dated anyone else."

"Oh my," I said. She was so young. She had her whole life ahead of her. If she was bored with the guy now, what would happen in ten years? Or even five? He wasn't likely to get more interesting. "You really should," I said, freely dispensing advice. Me, the relationship queen. "Even if it's just to make sure he's the right guy. You're too young to stay with someone you're not sure about."

"But everybody thinks we're perfect for each other," she said.

Isn't that always the way?

"It doesn't matter what everyone else thinks. It only matters what you think," I told her.

"But I don't *know* what I think. He's a really good guy and we have a lot in common. And our families are really good friends."

"Well, that's all very nice," I said in my new role as Dr. Phil, "but you're the one who's going to have to live with your decision."

"Yeah, yeah," she said. "I know. But I have to live with my family, too. What they think is important to me."

She turned her face back to the window, crying again. "He really is a good guy," she said without turning.

We arrived in Tampa a little early and I drummed my fingers on the armrest as we sat on the runway waiting for our gate to open. When we finally parked at the gate, passengers stood patiently in the aisles while my stomach fluttered. People who hadn't said a word to each other for two and a half hours now chatted amiably.

"Are you here for business or pleasure?"

"How long have you lived here?"

"Oh, you should try this great new restaurant while you're here. . . ."

"Really? What high school did you go to . . . ?"

The young woman in the window seat had packed up all of her little bags and zipped up her tapestry carry-on. She stood. She was less than five feet tall and fit neatly under the plane's low ceiling by the window.

"I hope you'll be happy whatever you decide to do," I said.

She nodded and smiled. "Me, too," she said. "But how do you ever know if you're doing the right thing?"

She was asking *me*? She had no idea who she was talking to.

"You don't," I said. "You just forge ahead and hope for the best."

❦

Finally we disembarked and I walked through the terminal, moving quickly past slow-moving families and dawdling travelers. Didn't they know I was in a hurry? As I got closer to the main terminal I saw people waiting ahead, just beyond security. The fluttery feeling in my stomach came back and I took a breath to calm myself.

I focused on a woman in front of me, her big butt jiggling softly underneath her silky floral-print skirt. Bad outfit. She should have worn something less clingy with a long jacket. I looked down at my own ensemble: gray pants, white blouse, black vest. Had I worn the right thing? Should I have worn something more feminine? More festive? More casual? Sexier? Oh god.

I squinted, looking ahead for someone with a handwritten sign, but didn't see him. Maybe he forgot. Or changed his mind. Maybe he had an accident on the way to the airport.

When I got past the security area I stood, searching the crowd, seeing some smiling faces, some anxious ones, occasional shouts of recognition, waving, hugging. But no Patrick.

I checked my cell phone but there was no message. No text. So I waited, tapping my foot, wondering what I'd do if he didn't show up. Perhaps he was waiting outside by the baggage claim area, but I worried that if I went down there he'd show up here and we'd miss each other. So I stayed put, trying to be patient. Not my strong suit.

I pulled out my compact and checked my reflection. My face was flushed and shiny, with fine wrinkles around my eyes and mouth that made me want to rush right out and get a shot of Botox. Since I couldn't do that I applied fresh lipstick, checked my hair, made sure nothing was hanging out of my nose or stuck in my teeth, and put the compact away. Then I heard someone shouting, "Libby!" and turned around to see Patrick weaving his way through the crowd, waving his sign. CARSON PARTY, it said, and I laughed out loud.

"I'm sorry I'm late," he said, standing in front of me looking casually handsome in jeans and a salmon-colored T-shirt.

I could feel my smile taking over my face. "It takes a real man to wear pink," I said.

He flexed his muscles. "You bet," he said, and grinned.

"For a minute there I thought you weren't coming."

"I know, I know. Traffic was nuts. I was going crazy." He wrapped me in a big bear hug, just as I'd imagined. "I'm so glad you're here," he whispered in my ear.

It felt good to be in his buoyant presence. He smelled of shampoo and a slightly spicy aftershave. His hair curled softly on his neck. So far so good, I thought. But who knows? Maybe by tomorrow we'd be on each other's nerves. Maybe I'd find out he chewed with his mouth open and belched at the dinner table. Maybe he spit in public. Maybe he was a total slob. Maybe he left the toilet seat up.

I laughed at my thoughts and Patrick pulled back and looked at me.

"What?" he said. His eyes sparkled, fine lines fanned out happily in the corners.

"Nothing," I said. "I'm just glad to see you."

He kissed me fully on the lips, a long, lingering, head-spinning kiss that made me feel seventeen. I felt the color rise to my cheeks. It reminded me of the excitement I'd felt when he kissed me so many years ago. It had made me tingle with the rightness of it. There was promise in the air back then, a promise unfulfilled. Maybe that was a little of what I was feeling now, even though I knew there was a huge chance it wouldn't work this time around either. But you never knew, did you?

His hand caressed my cheek as if it were made of the most delicate glass. "Come on," he said, taking the handle of my rolling bag in one hand and draping his other arm across my shoulder. "I promised you soft-shell crabs and drinks with umbrellas in them."

"On the beach?"

"Absolutely."

There would be waves lapping at the shore and the setting

sun painting the sky with shades of orange and red. We would toast to whatever this would be. Right this minute it felt so easy and right, like being on a picnic or playing catch in the backyard. But that could change in an instant. If I hadn't come to see him, though, I'd never know. And the thing is, there's no rewind button in life. If you don't take advantage of the opportunities when they present themselves, they're lost to you forever.

I couldn't help thinking of how Michael had looked on Wednesday as he left my house, the disappointment in his eyes, the straightness of his spine as he walked out, and it made me sad. The young woman on the plane had asked how you ever know if you're doing the right thing. I was surely the worst person in the world to answer that question but I thought my advice was valid: just make your best guess, forge ahead and hope for the best.

As we walked to Patrick's car I had a little fantasy of us sitting in front of a fireplace somewhere twenty years from now in matching La-Z-Boys, sipping steaming cups of tea, companionably reading the paper and glancing up occasionally to smile at each other. And then the warmth of the sun and the tantalizing pressure of his arm on my shoulder brought me back to the present. It was surreal to be walking by his side, and exhilarating, and I felt a gladness I hadn't felt in a long while. It made me appreciate that I still had an entire undiscovered life ahead of me.

Fifty wasn't a death sentence, it was just a number. Just a word. And it didn't have to be a holy-shit kind of word. I could still plant possibilities in the garden of my future. Some of them would take root, others would not, but nothing could grow if I didn't plant it there.

What I knew in that moment was that I would enjoy being with Patrick for as long as it would last: a day, a weekend, a lifetime. And if it didn't work out I would be fine. I didn't need another person to make me happy. Maybe love was in my future or maybe I'd depleted the relationships the universe had allotted me. Still, I had a good life, wonderful family and friends, a good job with interesting clients. I had Rufus. Maybe I'd get a dog. Maybe I'd sell my house and move downtown. Maybe I'd audition for *Project Runway*.

It was all out there if I wanted it.

I felt a lifting in my heart, and sighed. Patrick smiled down at me with such pleasure that it made me blush. "It's going to be a great weekend," he said, opening the door of his SUV.

He stashed my bag in the back and then climbed into the driver's seat. He put the key in the ignition and slapped the top of the steering wheel with both hands, a look of pure joy on his face. "Ready?" he asked.

I laughed. "Ready," I said.

Acknowledgments

I want to say thanks to Judi Tepe, my best friend, for her love, support, and encouragement all the years of our friendship (most of our lives). To all my "readers" over the years: many thanks for your thoughtful comments to Debby Keim, Barbara Hill, Jan Lewis, Teresa Borden, and especially Karen Gillis (oh man, I hope I haven't forgotten someone), and all the people in my various writing workshops whose names I don't remember but whose feedback was invaluable.

I have to acknowledge my favorite writers, even though you don't know who you are, because you've kept me entertained and inspired, you've struck me dumb with awe of your talent, and you've encouraged me to write without even knowing it. And to Mrs. Allen in third grade at Fulton School, who read my first short story aloud to the class and gave me an A+.

Many thanks to my editor, Brenda Copeland, who got me and the story I was telling, and to my copy editor, Sara Sarver, who saved me from certain embarrassment.

Thanks to my cousin Len for being inordinately proud of me, and thanks to Dave for inspiring this story.

And most of all, thanks to you, my readers.